ISBN: 978-1-943728-04-6
Published by Samantha Sabian and Arianthem Press
THE GODDESS OF THE UNDERWORLD Vol 8 CHRONICLES OF ARIAN-
THEM, 2016. FIRST PRINTING.
Office of Publication: Los Angeles, California

What did you think of this book? We love to hear from our readers.
Please email us at: samantha@arianthem.com.

THE GODDESS OF THE UNDERWORLD
THE CHRONICLES OF ARIANTHEM VIII

by Samantha Sabian

Chapter 1

aine opened her eyes.

Her body felt heavy, her limbs leaden. She was weak and she was in pain. Not a terrible pain, just a dull ache, as if she had been in a brutal fight. Her mind sought to identify where she was, how she had gotten here, but she could remember nothing. She was cold. She struggled to keep her eyes open, and slowly the room around her came into focus.

She was in a bed, a tangle of black silk sheets wrapped around her body. She was wearing a dark purple robe. A thought of her mother flitted through her muddled brain. The frame of the bed was odd, made of neither wood nor metal, but rather of black rock, like some natural formation. Somewhere near was the sound of water, a gentle flow. She tried to lift her head, but it was too heavy. She could see little else around her, so her eyes settled on the ceiling above.

Or what should have been a ceiling. The walls reached upward to where they ended in the night sky. It was disorienting to Raine. It was not as if the room was open to the night air; the chamber was large, but enclosed, almost cave-like. It was as if the ceiling was the night sky. Stars twinkled above her, and the vast panorama filled Raine with a strange, existential dread. These constellations were unfamiliar, the arrangement of stars foreign and unrecognizable. There were no accustomed landmarks, no established positions or angles. A feeling of despair flooded Raine, the despair of one who suddenly realizes they are far, far away from home. Her eyelids grew heavy, she lost the struggle to keep her eyes open, and she slowly drifted back into unconsciousness.

A few feet away, a demon watched the prone figure in a sullen manner. The handmaiden next to him, pale and coldly beautiful, also observed the brief return to consciousness. Her dark eyes flicked to her Mistress.

The Goddess of the Underworld sat near the bed on a black rock formation. The rock formation was fashioned into a throne-like couch lined with black silk cushions. Hel gazed at the figure in the bed in deep contemplation, her fingers slowly drumming a dirge on the arm rest. Both of her servants watched her closely, trying to glean a reaction from the brief stirring of her captive, but both were disappointed. The Goddess sat expressionless, unreadable, unmoved and unmoving, absorbed in her lengthy vigil. And although Feray and Faen agreed on little, they were united in a singular thought: neither had ever seen their Mistress so utterly and unconditionally patient.

Chapter 2

The dim light of the room began to pierce the total darkness behind her eyelids. Raine's eyes again fluttered open. Her body was still leaden, but her pain had lessened. She was cold, but the robe was snuggly wrapped around her form. The foreign stars twinkled mockingly overhead. She could move her head a little, and was able to raise up slightly. There was a pool of black water to her left, the smoothly banked cistern giving the impression of a bathing area. Water trickled down the rough rock wall, creating the sound she had heard earlier. An elaborate couch, or maybe it was a throne, sat empty, its design similar to the bed, made of black stone. Even that brief exertion exhausted her, and she lowered her head back to the silk pillow.

She stared up at the stars. Where was she? What was this strange place? And where was—?

Weynild.

It all came rushing back to her. The battlefield, the army of Hyr'rok'kin, a million strong. The allied forces, elves, dwarves, imperials, the Ha'kan, the Tavinter, all stood ready to fight. The dragons had not yet come. Hel appeared before Raine, and Weynild, her dragon lover, had tried to come to her aid, passing through Nifelheim...

Raine closed her eyes. And fallen into a trap. Raine had heard the dragon's cries and followed her into Nifelheim, goaded by the taunts of the Goddess. But she had never found her love. She could only hear her cries of pain, then was in her own battle with a horde of demons. She had slain dozens, possibly hundreds, but was overwhelmed by sheer numbers and went down in a swarm. The last thing she remembered was that she was being beaten to death.

Faen, his red eyes glittering with malice, saw the expression on the mortal's face and, like all despair, it filled him with glee. He ambled over in his sideways, loping manner and peered down into the beautiful face he already hated. His approach had been silent, but the blue and gold markings rose on her skin. Her eyes reopened.

Raine stared into the ugly, impish face of the demon. His skin was dark maroon, wrinkled, and he had two little horns like those on a young goat. His tail moved around behind him like a separate entity. Right now it hovered cautiously, poised as if it were more afraid of the creature in the bed than was the demon himself. Raine turned away, dismissing him.

The demon was infuriated. The arrogance of this one would not stand.

"You're going to get what's coming to you very soon."

The raspy voice of the demon barely registered on Raine in her weakened state, and she did not respond. This angered the fiend even more.

"The Goddess will rape you, and when she is through with you, she will give you to us."

Raine stared up at the stars, bored. Her insouciance enraged him, and the volume of his voice rose with her lack of reaction.

"The Goddess always quickly tires of her toys!" he said, spitting with his rage. "When she is done with you, she will toss you into the arena where you will be raped by multitudes! Garmr will go to work on you with his great tongue, then mount you from behind!"

This caught Raine's attention, not because of the demon's disgusting histrionics, but because it told her where she was. Garmr was the bloodstained watchdog that guarded the Underworld, which meant that she was now in the heart of Hel's realm. This thought affected her far more profoundly than all of the demon's frenzied, sickening threats, and she fought the return of the despair. The demon thought that he had at last scored a victory, but when the mortal responded, her tone was utterly calm.

"Strange," Raine began, and the demon leaned forward to hear her weak voice. "Strange, that you have known Hel for eons, and I, but hours…"

The demon leaned closer so he could catch the words.

"And yet already I know her better than you."

The fiend exploded, dancing and hopping about in fury, but Raine had turned her head away from him, and before he even finished his jig of wrath, she had already fallen back asleep.

Chapter 3

The third time Raine awoke, there was no comfortable period of memory loss. She knew exactly where she was as she stared up at the alien stars. Her limbs were once again heavy and her body was very, very cold. She sensed something else in the room, something far more dangerous than that foolish little demon, something of which she was genuinely afraid.

The Goddess moved to where Raine could see her, flowing with a malign and sensual grace. She stared down at her captive, the glittering emerald eyes assessing the chiseled features, the dark blue eyes, the clenched fists that corded the forearms, further emphasizing the blue and gold markings that stood in bold relief on that lovely skin.

"You know," the Goddess said casually, "I thought that I would be able to wait." Her hand drifted down to the muscular leg that lie partially exposed from beneath the robe. She stroked the skin, that mesmerizing combination of firmness beneath softness that was irresistible. Raine looked away from her, desperately trying to maintain control.

"I thought I would be able to defer my pleasure, to delay my gratification."

The hand drifted upward, moving beneath the robe as Hel settled onto the bed beside her. "But I was wrong." The hand settled between Raine's legs possessively, causing Raine to stifle a gasp. It did not move as the Goddess continued her casual conversation.

"Did you know that Arlanians can be forced to climax against their will?"

Raine stared up at the stars. "It is well-known," she said through clenched teeth, "that even the most inept lover can make an Arlanian come."

Hel would not allow her to distance herself from the doomed, beautiful people. "Can make you come," she reminded her. The hand moved ever-so-slightly and Raine muffled a moan of anguish as the Goddess continued, "and you and I both know that I am not an inept lover."

This last was a pronouncement of Raine's fate as the hand began its gentle stroking.

"Look at me," Hel commanded, and Raine obeyed. Despite the immobilizing control the Goddess was exerting over her, her hips twitched beneath the softly stroking hand. Hel felt the beginnings of the response, and saw the dark blue eyes begin to fleck with violet.

"Ah, there we are."

And Raine understood what the Goddess was doing. The blue and gold markings on her arms were slowly fading. All of her strength, all of her will, every part of her that was Scinterian was disappearing into the violet of her eyes. Had Hel taken her forcefully, it would have triggered a response that would have kept her Scinterian side at least present. But this gentle, skilled seduction was terrible. Everything that was strong in her was dwindling until only the Arlanian remained. And Hel knew it.

"No," Raine said, turning her head away.

"Oh yes," Hel said as she reached down and turned Raine's chin back to face her. The stroking of the hand continued, but it had done its work. The purple of those eyes was fabulous.

The hand stopped, and Raine knew that her fate was sealed. The Goddess leaned down to kiss her.

For Hel, the touch of those lips was extraordinary. Those who had never experienced an Arlanian before had no idea the ecstasy these creatures produced. Their smell was intoxicating, the taste of their skin was delightful, just touching them produced pleasure so profound that lesser beings might climax instantly. But Hel was not a lesser being and her hands went beneath the robe as she continued the kiss, her tongue probing deeply. She would not risk removing her own robes, for her nipples were already straining the silken confines of their bodice. There would be plenty of time for that later. No, this was about something else.

Raine bit off another moan that was part anguish, part pleasure. The kiss moved to her neck and throat area while the hands caressed her breasts and stomach. Her hips betrayed her as they sought to press against the Goddess, and it was only Hel's restraint of her that kept her from doing so. The kiss traveled down to the breasts, toying with the nipples, playfully suckling while one hand moved back between her legs. Hel enjoyed the coolness of the Arlanian's skin, which although had warmed with blood flow, still was pleasantly cold. The kiss trailed down the ridged muscles of the stomach, the lips feathering the taut muscles there.

Raine looked down at the progress of the head, knowing that all was lost. Hel sensed her captive's imminent defeat, and looked up to give her one last triumphant stare. And then she bent her head back down, and those lips settled on the soft, throbbing wetness beneath her.

Something inside of Raine exploded and she saw stars, although not those on the ceiling above her. The tongue and lips of the Goddess were merciless as the mouth drove her to orgasm. The mouth was hungry, rapacious, and either Hel had released her control of Raine or Raine had overcome it, for her hips thrust and writhed upward at the Goddess' command. The climax was endless, wave-after-wave of crushing pleasure, every muscle in her body straining to sustain the peak until at last a final peak crashed down upon her. This final wave satisfied her and perhaps saved her, because she might not have stopped until her body ripped apart.

Hel smiled and wiped her mouth on the silken sheets. She had forgotten how good Arlanians tasted. She glanced up at the sleeping, angelic face, her prisoner having already slipped back into exhausted sleep. This one was even stronger than she had anticipated; even wounded she had managed a climax nearly unmatched in Hel's considerable history.

"You are mine now," she whispered.

The Goddess stood, enjoying for a moment the sight of her conquered enemy lying naked in her bed. She composed herself, thoughtful.

Faen, on the other hand, was flabbergasted as he stared from the shadows of his alcove. By all that was dark and unholy, what had that been? He had expected violence, force, humiliation—not whatever that was. His Mistress had not even climaxed herself, merely pleased the woman. He examined Hel. Although, he had to admit, he had never seen such a look of satisfaction on his Queen's face before. He turned his attention back to the prone figure and smiled wickedly. Now this would be good.

The Membrane floated in from the balcony. The creature was a horrific amalgamation of body parts: breasts, vaginas, phalluses, testicles, anuses, mouths, and lips, all sexual organs that continually kissed, licked, sucked, and penetrated one another. The monstrosity, made up of souls whom Hel had cursed or whom the creature had seduced, was in a state of continual, painful orgasm. It was drawn to sexual energy, and it hovered above the comatose figure in the bed in a frenzy of anticipation. Lips smacked, a phallus grew erect, nipples hardened, and the abomination sought to settle upon its prey.

"No!" Hel said sharply. She had caught sight of the creature out of the corner of her eye. "You will not touch her."

The Membrane whipped about in agony, but it would not dare disobey the Goddess. It darted to-and-fro, then flitted out onto the balcony from which it came.

Hel turned to her Chief familiar.

"No one touches her," the Goddess commanded. "No one but me." The comatose figure in the bed shivered slightly, and her skin had taken on a bluish hue at the presence of the Membrane. Hel waved her hand imperiously and flame exploded in every sconce, bowl, decanter, lamp and alcove in the room. A spiral of hundreds of lit candles surrounded the bed, and the room was awash in flame as the flickering light cast ominous shadows on the wall.

"And keep her warm," she said dismissively as she left the room.

Faen stared after his Mistress in stunned disbelief. He turned to the despised figure in the bed, trying to fathom this unprecedented series of events. His only saving grace was that the Arlanian was unconscious, and therefore could not hear how right she had been.

The dim light again pierced the veil of Raine's unconsciousness and her eyelids fluttered open. She was cold, but not as cold as before since she was now surrounded by fire. And she was wearing clothing, not just the robe, but rather a simple shirt and pants combination made of dark lavender silk, something to lounge around in. This thought was grimly humorous to her: casual wear for the Underworld. She sat up in bed, then threw her legs over the side so that her feet were on the ground. She ran her fingers through her hair, staring at the smooth black floor in contemplation.

She became aware of some rather intense scrutiny and looked up to see the Goddess watching her intently from a table across the room. Raine inwardly cursed herself; none of her instincts seemed to work in this place. She returned Hel's gaze steadily, then let her eyes drift to those serving the Goddess. Hel was surrounded by voluptuous women in various states of dress, or perhaps undress was the better term as most were scantily clad and several were nearly naked. All were beautiful and Raine paid them not the slightest attention, a fact that both the Goddess and Feray noted.

Raine sighed and looked down at the ground once more. Hel made an imperious gesture to Feray, and the handmaiden rose to obey. Raine looked up as she approached. This one was older than the rest, slightly older in appearance than even Hel herself, and she wore robes like the Goddess, giving an impression of dignity and grace rather than the carnal servility of the others. She did not speak, but made a gesture toward the table. Feray wondered if the Arlanian would be so foolish as to disobey the Goddess, and she was relieved when, after a slight hesitation, the woman merely sighed again and got to her feet.

Raine padded across the black floor barefoot. The floor was warm, as was the entire room, which became noticeable as Raine approached the table, because her body temperature dropped as her proximity to the Goddess increased. She stood before Hel with her eyes downcast, not out of subservience but because she feared her eyes would turn violet if she looked upon her.

"Sit."

It was not an offer but a command, and like all of Hel's commands, it was also a veiled threat. Every decree she issued held the promise of punishment at disobedience. Raine sat down.

The table was filled with food: fruits, meats, pastries, bread, cheese, vegetables, an exotic array of colors, textures, and smells. Much of the food Raine had never seen before. Despite the sumptuous buffet, Hel seemed content to sip her wine while she watched the creature across from her. She wondered if the Arlanian would ask any of the questions she knew must be burning within her, specifically, the fate of all that she loved.

She did not. Instead, she made a simple observation.

"I did not realize the gods ate food."

Hel smiled. "The gods have all the appetites of mortals. Where do you think you got them?"

This conversation was already veering into uncomfortable territory for Raine. "But you do not require food to survive?"

"No." Hel's eyes lingered on the lips of her captive. "I have all of your appetites, none of your needs."

This silenced Raine. Apparently any conversation with the Goddess was going to be dangerous.

"Eat."

Feray again watched the Arlanian for any sign of defiance. It was unheard of for any to sit in the presence of the Queen, let alone dine with her at her table. Feray was not certain the Arlanian understood the honor that had been bestowed upon her, or that she even cared. The handmaiden released her breath when the woman acquiesced, choosing a bright red berry and biting into it experimentally.

Raine was surprised at the juicy flavor of the fruit. It was difficult to describe, both sweet and tart with traces of spice. She perused the table in front of her and chose another which was just as delightful. She pondered the strange, purple berry, wondering what kind of tree or bush it had come from. And, absorbed in her reflection on the food, she was oblivious to the attention she was attracting.

The handmaidens were enamored with this creature. She was physically imposing, lithely muscular, deadly agile. And yet when she sat at the table, it was as if she turned into another person. She moved gracefully, almost delicately, with a sensual grace. Every tilt of her head, every brush of her hair, every pensive bite of her lip, every unconscious gesture was imbued with a mesmerizing sensuality that somehow also conveyed a sense of innocence. They watched greedily as she bit into the berry, unable to look away from that mouth even though their scrutiny could bring them death.

Feray was not immune to the Arlanian's charm, either, but possessed a poise that had kept her alive in the Queen's service longer than any. She was aware of the scrutiny of the handmaidens, and the only thing that was saving them right now was the fact that the Goddess was so absorbed in the Arlanian herself that she had not noticed. Her eyes continued to linger on those lips in a manner that told Feray it was time for them to leave. She gestured impatiently to the ogling women, who broke themselves from their spell and hurriedly exited.

The abrupt departure of the handmaidens made Raine uneasy and her eyes flicked back to the Goddess, which was a mistake for Hel's marked observation only increased her unease and brought a flicker of purple to her eyes. She set the remains of the berry down and stared at the table in front of her.

"You should eat," Hel said.

Raine knew that she should not disobey her, but pushed away from the table anyway. "I'm not hungry."

Feray looked to her Mistress, fearful what this act of defiance would bring. But the Goddess was only amused. She had seen the flash of violet in Raine's eyes, seen the flush of crimson in her cheeks, understood completely the agitation that had flustered the Arlanian and sent her fleeing across the room. It was all the more entertaining because there was nowhere she could go. Raine had turned her back on the Goddess which sent her toward the bed, a most dangerous direction she realized once halfway there. An awkward stutter step communicated that realization and made Hel nearly laugh out loud. Raine moved towards a balcony as the closest means of escape.

But it was not a means of escape. Raine stared out over a vast, subterranean hall, its walls disappearing into the darkness above. Below her, an enormous staircase led up to a ghastly and magnificent throne. The hall itself was populated by a curious mixture of beings: demons, demi-gods, sprites and other supernatural creatures that Raine could not identify. And intermixed with these beings were spirit-like figures that flickered in and out, moving amongst the crowds and sometimes right through them.

"This is my court."

The low voice in her ear made Raine start. The Goddess was standing right behind her, looking over her shoulder, so close that the breath on the back of her neck made her skin tingle.

"It is where I sit in judgment."

"And is this where you will judge me?"

The bitter question was out of her mouth before she could stop herself, and Raine knew that it was a mistake.

"Judge you?" Hel said, turning her chin so that Raine was forced to look up at her. "No, you will not be judged. Your fate has already been decided."

Hel leaned down and captured her mouth in a kiss, and Raine felt the familiar despair. Her inability to resist, her uncontrolled response, her apparent unwillingness to fight, borne of the Arlanian passivity that took hold when the beautiful people understood they were in a hopeless situation. Had Hel taken her violently or by force, she might have been able to resist, but she had no defense against Hel's gentle, indomitable seduction.

And the Goddess knew it. Her soft but firm touch was not from kindness, but from an ultimate cruelty. The fact that it brought her enormous physical pleasure was just an added benefit. Her kiss went deeper, and she turned the Arlanian by the shoulders, then pressed her backward against the wall. She trapped her hands against the stone and buried her tongue in that yielding mouth. A tortured noise came from Raine, and then she began to return the kiss. Hel was lost to the sensation, for there was nothing like the kiss of an Arlanian, especially this one. The tongue was so soft, so delightfully cool. She pulled back, pleased with the torment in those violet eyes.

"Let me show you your fate."

And then Raine was standing next to the bed, facing it, and the Goddess was behind her, hands around her waist. Hel kissed the back of her neck as she slowly pulled the loose shirt over her head. She nibbled on her ear and the breath was maddening to Raine, as were the hands that came around her front to caress her breasts. The hands dipped down, and then the pants were gone, dropped to the floor. Hel made her own robes disappear and pressed against that magnificent back, her nipples hardening as soon as they brushed that wonderful skin. To press against an Arlanian, skin-to-skin, was an extraordinary sensation that was indescribable.

And Hel had dreamed of this moment, when she would dominate this hybrid creature of myth. She guided the Arlanian face-down onto the bed, still kissing and biting her neck, rubbing up against the muscled buttocks and marveling at how good they felt between her legs. She could probably climax through that action alone, but she wanted far more than that. She ran her hands over that glorious back, unmarred by the defect of those blue and gold scars. It was a work of art, perfectly proportioned, supple and firm, with ideal musculature and structure.

Hel leaned back and the ebony phallus appeared in her hand, an object she gazed at with some entertainment. It had been a gift from Sjöfn, although truthfully, there was little love lost between her and the Goddess of Love. Sjöfn had given it to her years before, and the item possessed two unique blessings. First, it would take on the size and shape most appropriate for the one on the receiving end, so pain and dissatisfaction became unlikely. Second, it intensified the pleasure of the one on the giving end, based upon the amount of pleasure the receiver was experiencing.

It was an unsubtle criticism from Sjöfn, and Hel thought it a stupid gift. She cared nothing for the well-being of whatever vessel she chose to violate, so size had been irrelevant to her. And normally she cared little for their pleasure as well. Although the feedback potential of the device was intriguing, none felt pleasure as intensely as she, so their contributions to her orgasm were minimal. She intended to throw the "blessed phallus" away, as she had so sarcastically named it, but all of that had changed when she had seen the Arlanian for the first time through the eyes of the Membrane. To use it on such a beautiful creature, one who could not help but feel the most intense pleasure, now that would be glorious.

Raine braced herself for whatever was about to happen, for she felt Hel's hands on her hips, positioning her on the edge of the bed, the strength of the Goddess such that she moved her into place without effort. And the penetration came, the pleasure so intense with a single stroke that it nearly caused her to black out. She could not muffle the groan that escaped her lips.

And the Goddess had to stop, taking several quick breaths to regain control. The feeling of gliding into that slender Arlanian, of sliding into that superb wetness, with a stroke between those legs so smooth and firm and perfect, was beyond ecstasy. Hel had no words to describe what she was feeling, only that it was god-like in its intensity. She paused, gathered herself, then delivered another firm stroke that caused her beautiful captive to muffle another tortured noise.

The strokes continued, slowly, one after the other, with a pause in between, each gliding into the center of Raine's being, each touching her exactly where she needed to be touched with the perfect amount of pressure. At first the strokes were measured, methodical, as if the Goddess were teaching her a lesson, showing her the control she exerted over her, holding her hips still with her hands. But then the strokes grew faster, deeper, as if Hel had made her point and was now giving way to the storm of pleasure that was enveloping them both. Raine clutched the silken sheets, stuffing them into her mouth to keep from crying out. Hel leaned forward to bury the phallus deeper and to taste the salt on that beautiful back. She was no longer in any control and was riding a wave that might very well destroy her. The thrusts came faster and deeper and her hips ground into the slender mortal beneath her, wanting only to push her over the edge and then go with her.

And finally, Raine released, every muscle in her body tightening while endless spasms shook her inside. Hel also released, her orgasm shaking her to her core. She was so deep inside this gorgeous creature she felt as if they were one. She could feel the pulsations inside the body beneath her, and they matched her own. She collapsed on the exhausted Arlanian, who was already drifting into unconsciousness. Despite her own exhaustion, the feel of her full breasts on that strong back was delightful. She toyed with the damp hair at the nape of Raine's neck as she made the phallus disappear, then whispered in her ear.

"Now that is your fate, for all eternity."

Raine did not respond, and the Goddess rolled over, pulling the prone figure from her position half off the bed, a feat she accomplished with one hand. She rolled Raine over onto her side, then embraced her from behind, pressing her full length against that skin that was still so impossibly cool. She pulled the sheet over them both, fully sated and content, her arm around Raine's waist and her leg over her thigh. She began to drift off to sleep, sleep something she did not need, but right now, seemed highly desirable.

Feray watched her Mistress from the alcove. She had never, ever, seen Hel in the throes of passion in such a way, and she was quite certain the entire court had heard her cry "yes, yes" over and over again. Feray had also been quite certain the Arlanian would not survive the encounter, but the mortal was astonishingly resilient.

And this, Feray thought, examining Hel's intimate and possessive position with the mortal, this was entirely new. Hel had deigned to dine with but a few over Feray's very long period of service, but the handmaiden had never known her to sleep with anyone.

Chapter 4

The First General of the Ha'kan watched her First Ranger train on the archery range with a skill and concentration that was unsurpassed. Skye had always trained with focus and determination, but now she trained like one possessed. Those who had struggled to keep pace with her before now did not have a chance.

It had been four weeks since the Ceremony of Assumption, four weeks since they had fought a battle with the Hyr'rok'kin, thinking their triumph against the much larger force was a great victory, until one even larger arrived. It had been four weeks since Skye, back-to-back, lost two of the great loves of her life. Her great-grandfather, Isleif, the powerful but aged wizard had passed away in the Deep Woods, and Raine, Skye's beloved idol had been taken from Arianthem by the Goddess of the Underworld herself. And no one knew what had become of Talan, Raine's dragon lover.

Senta watched as Skye fired arrow after arrow at random targets, never missing. They all suffered, mourning the loss of Talan and Raine. The initial impulse had been to ride across the Empty Land, through the Veil, then on to the Gates of the Underworld itself, but the elven seer Y'arren had dissuaded them from such rash action. Despite their desperation, they listened to her, not simply because she was one of the oldest and wisest creatures in all of Arianthem, but also because she was Raine's godmother. No one mourned Raine's capture more than Y'arren, so if she urged caution, they obeyed.

There were things that had to be done, techniques that had to be learned, skills that had to be perfected. Skye was now working with Y'arren directly to learn to control the magic that flowed through her. The elven matriarch had come to the Ha'kan capital and taken up temporary residence to facilitate Skye's training. The Queen of the Ha'kan welcomed her and offered her housing in her personal forum, but Y'arren asked instead if she might stay in the royal gardens. Queen Halla fretted at such low accommodations, but Y'arren settled in a corner of the orchard in a simple tent, surrounded by a few servants and her favored apprentice, Elyara, completely content.

Senta turned her attention to another who practiced without ceasing. A raven-haired beauty cast powerful destructive spells at targets on another part of the training field. Idonea, the most powerful mage in Arianthem, also trained with a single-minded purpose at odds with her normal wild and carefree manner. But that was understandable, given that Isleif had been her mentor, Raine, one of her closest friends, and Talan, her mother. Although she expressed little of her mourning, it was evident to all that she suffered. Y'arren was also instrumental in her training, passing on Isleif's last instruction to his protégé since he was no longer able to do so. And Y'arren provided comfort to the dark-haired mage in a way that no one else could, her gentle wisdom a salve for Idonea's unseen wounds.

Chapter 5

Feyden stood on the terrace, the very same terrace that Raine had stood on and gazed out over Arianthem, his friend the first to see the clouds gathering in the Empty Land, the clouds that foretold her doom. The pessimistic thought irritated Feyden and he shook his head violently to dispel it. Raine had survived, that much had been confirmed by the young Tavinter leader, who was able to sense the life force of his friend. And the elven matriarch Y'arren had speculated that it was not Hel's intent to kill Raine, although she had hinted that Raine's fate might be far worse.

The fair-haired elf turned back into the library where Dagna and Lorifal were still hard at work. Y'arren had spoken of a plan, a plan that Isleif had passed on to her in the days before his death. The diminutive wood elf had not shared the ideas with anyone; there was too much risk that someone would betray the secret, even if by accident. Instead, Y'arren had set a series of events in motion, given everyone direction as to what they should do to prepare, then left for the land of the Ha'kan. All were grateful for her direction, for the activities she required jarred them out of their numbed state.

He, Dagna, and Lorifal had been tasked with recreating their trip to the Underworld in as much detail as they could remember. Dagna had already memorialized the epic quest in which they had accompanied Raine to shut the Gates of the Underworld in her poem, "The Dragon's Lover." But that had been a lyric, heroically romantic account, whereas what was needed now was a pure recount of strategic features. How long had it taken them to cross the Empty Land? How steep was the descent down into the Veil? What was the terrain like within that netherworld and what enemies occupied it? What was the actual size of the first, great gates that guarded the red and black courtyard? How big was that courtyard? And how big were the actual Gates of the Underworld, the ones that the Queen of all Dragons, Talan'alaith'illaria, had shut before?

As he rejoined his companions, he was surprised at how much they agreed on regarding something that had happened over two decades ago. But perhaps that was not unusual, Feyden mused, since the events of the quest had been burned in all of their minds, so vivid that it might as well have happened last week.

Chapter 6

The subtle cues of day and night were becoming more apparent to Raine. There was no actual day and night. Raine was not certain if the Underworld was deep underground, or if it was an entirely separate realm, or both. But it felt subterranean, cave-like, and it was always dim. At times, like right now, it was a little less dim, giving the impression of day.

Raine pushed the black silk sheets away, glancing around the room. For once it seemed she was alone, not being stalked by the Goddess or watched by that handmaiden or demon. She took the opportunity to examine her surroundings and got to her feet. There was food left out on the table, but she was not hungry. As she walked past, she ran her fingers over the throne-like couch that Hel often sat upon, the soft silken cushions atop what looked like smoothly polished lava. The slow trickle of water in the bathing area continued its soft song. Across the room, the balcony which led to Hel's court was open, but Raine did not wish to step out there again. It was possible that Hel sat on that throne at the moment, and she did not want to catch her eye.

There was an arch to the right of the bathing area that led into an adjacent room, one that drew Raine's curiosity. The room was large, the ceiling higher than that in the bedroom, and the walls were not parallel, but rather slanted so that they were closer together at the far end, giving the room a sense of distorted perspective that made it feel even larger. It seemed some sort of ceremonial place, and each wall was covered with a huge curtain. The curtains felt ominous and as Raine stood before them, a chill went down her spine. She reached out to move the curtain aside, but could not even budge the heavy drape. The unexpected weight of the material and the strange disquiet it caused her gave her pause, and she stood in front of the coverings for some time. When at last she turned back into the room, Feray was looking at her. Raine was not certain if she was doing something wrong, but Feray did not say anything, so Raine walked toward her. She glanced down at the sleepwear in which she was clothed.

"Where is my armor?"

"It has been destroyed."

Feray made a motion with her hand, ignoring Raine's clenched jaw. Several of Hel's handmaidens appeared, bearing beautiful Arlanian clothing.

"And if I choose not to wear this?"

"There is no choice. The Goddess commands it." Feray paused, then added, "Although, I'm sure she would allow you to go naked."

Feray's tone was impassive but the sarcasm was evident, and the handmaidens bearing the clothing made it clear what their choice would be. Raine put out her hand to take the clothes.

"I can dress myself."

"You will not," Feray said in the same imperative tone. It was not open for discussion.

"Fine," Raine said, holding out her arms and allowing the women to dress her. Feray watched the process with a jaded eye. The hands of the servants lingered inappropriately, taking liberties which would get them killed sooner or later. The Arlanian, however, did not respond, simply stared at the wall in resigned silence. This fact pleased Feray, for it seemed the Arlanian's weakness was only for the Goddess. Her eyes remained ice-blue the entire time she was fondled by the voluptuous women hanging off her.

"Enough," Feray said, stopping the endless adjustment to the clothing which fit the Arlanian perfectly. She dismissed the handmaidens.

Raine stared down at the clothes, trying not to despise them. She had always worn the raiment of her mother's people in celebration. Now the clothes seemed to weigh as heavily on her as those massive curtains.

"What is beyond there?" Raine asked, nodding at a second balcony on the opposite side of the room as the first.

"You may go look."

Raine exited onto the balcony gingerly, lest she was walking into another throne room. But this balcony led to a vast space, one so vast it gave the impression of outdoors much like the dim light gave the impression of day. It was a garden, filled with darkly beautiful plants and trees. Fireflies and glowing moths flitted to-and-fro from strange, lovely flowers. Small animals grazed in the dark grass, their fluorescent markings magical in the picturesque gloom.

"This is Hel's private garden. It is forbidden to almost all."

"And me?" Raine asked.

"You are permitted."

Raine was certain she would pay for whatever privileges were afforded her so she might as well take advantage of them. She walked down the marble staircase to the grounds below.

It truly was an extraordinary garden. There were some flowers she recognized, nightshade, jasmine, evening primrose, and many others she did not. The air was heavy with the scent of the blossoms. Nightingales sang prettily to one another, perched upon the dark moss on the trees, and Raine thought she heard a reed warbler. Feray walked a short distance behind her.

"What is out there?" Raine asked. There was an abrupt drop-off of the garden into total darkness, a demarcation so evident it might as well have been a wall.

"Nothing," Feray said, and Raine cocked her head at her sideways. It was not an evasion, but rather a statement of fact.

"When I say nothing," Feray continued, "I mean nothingness, an emptiness so total that even the gods avoid it."

"Has anyone ever gone in there?" Raine asked curiously.

"Some have wandered away never to return. Those few beings strong enough to withstand the void all went mad. One of Hel's most trusted advisors returned from that darkness and now lies chained to a pillar, little more than a raving lunatic."

"Hmm," Raine said, then continued on with her exploration. At the far end of the garden she could see a tree, a hideous, twisted monstrosity that for some reason compelled her approach. Despite the forbidding appearance, her footsteps gave in to the compulsion and she was drawn toward the tree.

She stood before it and it glowed with a low amber light, emitting a humming sound. There was a gash in the bark that dripped a dark yellow sap, and Raine, fascinated, leaned forward to touch her finger to it.

"It's beautiful, is it not?"

Raine jumped, startled and blew out a breath of cold air. The Goddess was right behind her. She withdrew her hand.

"Yes," Raine said stiffly, "it is surprisingly lovely."

The admission pleased Hel, and she took it as perhaps a mandate on other things. Raine, who was involuntarily honest, perhaps meant it that way as well.

"It is the Tree of Death," Hel explained, plucking a leaf from a branch, "the twin of the Tree of Life which grows in the garden of Iðavöllr. It was grown by my head gardener, who walks this way."

Raine turned her attention to the strange being coming towards them, a man much like the spirit beings she had seen in Hel's court. He was nearly transparent, shimmering and shifting in the dim light, and Raine could see the flowers behind him by looking right through him. He muttered to himself, either unconcerned or oblivious to them, and Raine braced herself because he was going to walk right into her.

Instead, he passed right through her. She turned, astonished, as he continued on unimpeded.

"He walks in the realm of the dead," Hel said, "and although you can see and hear him, he cannot see or hear you. He is barely aware, even of me, unless I enter that realm."

"How did he wind up here?" Raine asked, wholly forgetting she was speaking to her mortal enemy.

"The dead are distributed according to their lives. The good go to Iðavöllr, the valiant go to the Holy Mountain, all others come to me."

"So he was evil?"

"Worse," Hel said, "he was mediocre. I judge them the harshest."

"So the creatures in your court, not all of them are dead?"

"Most of them are not dead. The spirits you saw, like him, are dead, moving about in their parallel realm. But my court is made up of demons, demi-gods, an entire pantheon of those who would court my favor."

"And your handmaidens?"

"Flesh and blood. My personal creations," Hel said, "like the Hyr'rok'kin."

The mention of the Hyr'rok'kin silenced Raine and she silently chewed her lip, the unconscious act so sensual the Goddess thought about taking her beneath the tree.

"Wait a minute," Raine said, turning back to look at the gardener who was floating ephemerally across the flower beds. "He passed right through me."

"Yes," Hel said, as if that were obvious.

Raine looked down at her hands, turning them over. "I'm not dead," she said slowly, "I'm not dead."

"Of course you're not dead."

Raine still stared at her hands as if they were new and wondrous appendages. "But why am I not dead?"

"Do you want me to kill you?" Hel asked.

"No," Raine said quickly. "No, it's not that. But why? Why didn't you kill me?"

The green eyes glowed. "A simple answer. There was no need. You entered Nifelheim of your own free will; death was unnecessary."

"And what is the more complicated answer?"

"Because I don't want you dead," Hel said. "The dead are subjugated to my will. You would slowly lose all independence and become little more than a thrall to me. And that is not what I want from you."

Raine suddenly understood the fate that had been handed to her, but Hel made it explicit.

"I enjoy your struggle. Subjugating a thrall is nothing, but subjugating you is divine."

It was a devastating pronouncement. Still, it seemed there was something Hel was withholding, as if she were debating saying more, but decided against it. And the pronouncement did not bother Raine nearly as much as it should have, rather she stood silently mulling the revelation. She did not resist when the Goddess motioned for her to accompany her, rather fell in beside her, intensely preoccupied.

The preoccupation annoyed Hel. She would rather face the Arlanian's fury than her disinterest. And the fact that Raine's eyes were violet and that Hel was likely not the cause stoked her anger. Both Faen and Feray observed the entrance of the Goddess with great misgiving. Faen was infuriated because the mortal walked at the side of the Goddess as an equal rather than behind her as she should. Feray, on the other hand, was dismayed by the unconscious disregard of the mortal; Hel had killed for far less. She stepped forward.

"Your Majesty, we have readied your bath."

All of the attention of her voluptuous attendants meant nothing to Hel at the moment, but that was not Feray's intent. She knew of the Arlanian's weakness for the Goddess and would exploit it. As the robes of the Goddess came off, the eyes of the Arlanian flicked upward, settling with involuntary intensity upon the curves of the sensual Queen. And as Hel settled into the bath, the water not quite covering her large, beautiful breasts, Feray breathed an inward sigh of relief, for the Arlanian's renewed attention instantly altered the mood of her Mistress.

Raine wanted to look away, but the ministrations of the hands of the attendants as they stroked and caressed that pale skin were mesmerizing. Fingers dipped beneath the water to stroke, lips feathered a kiss on that long neck, a mouth settled on one breast, and the emerald eyes of the Goddess were focused only on Raine. Raine could feel her heart pound in her chest, for she was more afraid of the desire that Hel inspired in her than any pain she might inflict. And Hel knew this, a slow smile curving about her face as she relished her captive's distress.

"Come here."

Raine could not move. She wanted to flee, to run into the garden, past the demarcation that led into oblivion, into the darkness from which she would never return. But she could not budge, uncertain if Hel was restraining her or if she had simply frozen. Normally, such resistance would have infuriated the Goddess, but Hel was only amused by the Arlanian's continued struggle, perhaps because it was so futile.

Feray approached Raine, taking the arm of the benumbed woman and gently leading her to the edge of the bath. Two attendants flowed upward from the water and skillfully removed Raine's clothing while Raine's eyes were imprisoned by those of the Goddess. And the Goddess released that gaze only to look at the beauty of that magnificent body. She had seen the Arlanian prone, she had seen her face-down in the bed in front of her, but she had not seen her standing upright in all her glory. The muscled splendor of that physique was jaw-dropping, and the hands of her attendants slowed, then stopped as they, too, stared in wonder and lust.

"Leave us."

The command of the Goddess produced anguish in the handmaidens, for Hel rarely banished them from her bedroom, and never had they desired so much to stay. But they were not so foolish as to linger, and Feray expedited their exit with furious motions.

"Come here," the Goddess repeated, and held out her hand.

Raine was still frozen, standing on the edge of the bath, gazing at the hand in tortured silence. Her heart was pounding so hard she was certain Hel could hear it, or at least see it as it beat against her chest wall. And slowly, she raised her hand and took that of the Goddess.

Hel pulled her gently forward on to her lap so that they were face-to-face. The water around the Arlanian cooled to a delightful temperature. Hel took a moment to gaze into eyes so purple they were nearly black. Then she kissed her prisoner, reveling in the tormented noise she elicited. And it was only a brief second before the Arlanian was kissing her back.

And that was something else that few understood. Arlanians could be forced into sexual enjoyment, pleasure could be taken from them at will. But if they were seduced rather than forced, gently and skillfully guided, they were as compelled to give pleasure as they were to receive it. And Hel felt that compulsion take hold of the lithe creature on her lap, as the hand hovered, trembled over her breast, shaking with a desire that all the strength in the world could not contain. And the hand surrendered, settling onto the breast with a caress that stole Hel's breath away. And where the hand went, the lips followed, and that beautiful mouth took the nipple, then as much of the breast as it could, kissing, and licking and suckling with a longing that nearly brought the Goddess to climax just watching. Hel shifted up the slope of the pool so that most of her body was out of the water, and the Arlanian did not hesitate, kissing every inch of her stomach, her ribs, her abdomen, her hip, then trailing lower. The warm water lapped against her sides as that beautiful little mouth settled between her legs and Hel closed her eyes, then stared at the ceiling in disbelief. Her dark green eyes returned to the creature between her legs, however, because she had dreamed of this moment and the sight of the Arlanian going down on her gave her as much pleasure as the sensation of those lips on the center of her being. The gentleness of the feathery kiss, a stark contrast to the muscles that bulged and bunched as they held the thighs, drove Hel mad. She had no control and wanted none. Her hips moved with abandon as her fingers tangled in that fair hair and her feet pressed downward so her hips could move upward, and the Arlanian helped her by hooking those strong arms beneath her thighs, both opening her legs further and cradling her hips, causing her to explode in release. And somehow that beautiful little mouth stayed on her as she thrashed beneath the onslaught, never losing its rhythm as the Goddess of the Underworld came again and again in response to that insistent pressure.

Hel collapsed, her breath coming in gasps, her breasts heaving as her hardened nipples pointed to the night sky. The Arlanian also collapsed, barely able to pull herself up to rest her head on Hel's stomach. Although she had not climaxed, contact with Goddess, especially skin-to-skin, was exhausting for her, and sexual congress with her was as draining as fighting that legion of demons. She tried to stay conscious, but she could not and drifted into darkness.

Hel intertwined her fingers in the damp hair, caressing the smooth cheek that was still cool to the touch. The feeling and sight of that angelic face lying on her stomach filled Hel with pleasure. She had not been so satisfied in bed since this girl's dragon lover had brought her to orgasm eons ago. But as enjoyable as it had been, it made Hel thoughtful. Although the Arlanian had been on her knees, tortured by her own lack of self-control, the act had been anything but subservient. That had been nothing like the services provided by her minions, where Hel took whatever pleasure she felt was her due. Rather the Arlanian controlled her completely, driven to provide pleasure and doing so flawlessly. That could become dangerous.

And, Hel had to admit as she brushed the blonde hair from the cheek, part of her great joy was bringing this Arlanian to climax against her will, the mortal's loss of control driving her own. As enjoyable as that had just been, it was not what pleased her the most.

Sometime later, Raine awoke in the semi-darkness that indicated a nocturnal period in the land of perpetual darkness. She was alone in the black bed, wrapped in the satin sheets, surrounded by lit candles and a fire that burned in a nearby fireplace. The flames cast eerie shadows on the walls, intimating the demons that likely surrounded her, unseen. She pulled the sheets close, for even with the fire, she was chilled. She turned on her side and buried her face in the pillow, curling herself into a fetal position.

Despite the hopelessness of her position, the desperate futility of any action, her uncontrolled and humiliating response to the Goddess, Raine held one thing very close to her heart. It was what had distracted her earlier and caused her eyes to turn violet with merely its thought. It was something that warmed her even in her ice-cold prison, a life-line thrown into the despair that threatened to drown her. She was bound to her love, Weynild, which meant that her soul could not leave the mortal realm without her.

Which also meant, if Raine was not dead, then Talan'alaith'illaria, Queen of All Dragons, was still alive.

Chapter 7

erthus watched the Empress and her great-grandchildren. It was a strangely conventional scene given the utter dysfunction and weirdness that had precipitated it. Aesa had appeared right after Raine had been taken by the Goddess, demanding that the Emperor, her grandson, relinquish the throne to her. Under other circumstances, the appearance of an Empress long thought dead, especially one who had not aged a day in two generations, might have given Nerthus and her fellow Knight Commander, Bristol, more pause. But Aesa had arrived just as the Emperor was backing away from his allies in an embarrassing display of cowardice, declaring that, not only would he not assist in rescuing Raine and Talan, but that he would prevent anyone else from doing so. Both Knight Commanders had been prepared to commit treason to remove him from the throne when Aesa had arrived and saved them the trouble.

And now, an undead Empress sat on the throne, shadowed by her vampyr lover Malron'a, once thought to be the Emperor's closest advisor, now revealed to be the assassin sent to kill Aesa so many years ago. And Nerthus had a feeling that "Malron'a" was not the vampyr's real name, nor was she any ordinary assassin. She felt an unease around the woman she felt around few.

It was all very confusing and unsettling for Nerthus, who thrived on structure and order. But Aesa had proven surprisingly adept as Empress, making numerous decisions regarded as both shrewd and diplomatic. Discovering that she had great-grandchildren, she had them brought before her and was pleased to learn they were nothing like her grandson. Perhaps this was because they had been raised entirely by their mother, who was little more than a girl herself. Malron'a suggested that the former Empress, displaced by Aesa, was not the "sharpest arrow in the quiver," and was little threat to her. So Aesa kept both mother and children in the palace with her, and none of the three seemed to miss the former Emperor, or really even notice that he was gone. And when Aesa appeared in the court accompanied by her great-grandchildren and the former Empress, all who seemed to adore her, it gave her claim to the throne a legitimacy that force alone would not have produced.

As so many others did, Nerthus raised her eyes to the larger-than-life portrait of Aesa on the wall. It had been painted right before her disappearance, in the bloom of her youth, and it was startling how much Aesa still looked like the young woman in the picture. Nerthus turned her attention back to the domestic scene, utterly tranquil save for the dark-robed woman in the background, hovering in the shadows like some great raven.

Nerthus sighed. The vampyr's presence had one distinct advantage. It fully freed both Nerthus and Bristol to prepare the imperial forces for the assault on the Underworld, for nothing would happen to Aesa or her offspring as long as Malron'a was near.

Chapter 8

Raine sat at the table drinking a cup of something hot. It was not tea, but something thicker and darker. And it had an almost bitter taste that was abolished with a little milk and sugar, turning the drink pleasant. She nibbled at a piece of bread, but was not really hungry. She wondered if her appetite and her need for food were affected by this place. She had no idea how long she had been there, but she had eaten very little the entire time. Yet she had rarely felt hungry and felt no loss of strength for the lack of sustenance.

"Good," Feray said as she glided into the room. "You're awake."

Feray came from the balcony leading to the throne room. There were only three entrances to Hel's chambers, one that led to the garden, one that led to the throne room, and another that came in from a hall. Raine was certain of this, for she had examined every inch of the series of rooms, seeking any means of escape. But there was only the garden, which was surrounded on all sides by that ominous oblivion, the throne room, which was heavily occupied at all times, and the hall, which was blocked by a heavy door that Raine could not budge. There were many hallways branching off from the throne room, but Raine surmised she had zero chance of reaching them undetected, and the Goddess seemed to know where she was at all times. Raine had left Hel's chambers only to walk in the garden, which she did often.

A throng of Hel's handmaidens followed Feray, bearing beautiful clothing: pants, a flowing shirt, soft boots, a cape. Raine looked at the clothing with distaste. It seemed Hel had gone to great lengths to discover all the fashions of the Arlanians, and enjoyed having her clothed in them. It was of no consolation that they were well-made, of the finest material, comfortable, and that she looked astonishing in them, a fact that the hand-maidens more than adequately expressed in their sighs of pleasure at her appearance.

"You will put these on."

Raine stood and held out her arms. She had given up resisting Feray. Any signs of rebellion from her were treated as the foolish tantrums of a child, and, out of sight of the Goddess, Feray would allow the wandering hands of the other handmaidens to linger for an extended period of time. Raine had learned that if she simply allowed them to dress her quickly, Feray would not let them touch her.

"That's enough," Feray said, motioning the handmaidens to step back. Their disappointment was evident, but at least they were allowed to look, for the Arlanian was particularly gorgeous in this raiment. Even Faen could not deny her exquisite appearance as he ambled sideways into the room, officious and overbearing as always.

"Hmph," he said in disgust, "that will have to do."

Feray was not fooled by the dismissal. The demon could not hide his emotions, and he was stunned, angry, jealous, and impressed all at the same time. She was beginning to enjoy the power this Arlanian wielded over her fellow familiar.

Although Raine yielded to Feray for the sake of expediency, she did not yield to Faen at all. Her disdain for the demon was evident, and it ran-kled him. The majority of time, she ignored him completely, which is what she was doing now. It was clear they were preparing her for something, and the limits of her patience and her cooperation were nearly at an end.

Faen pulled a scroll out of thin air and fluttered it in her face in a haughty manner. "Today, you will be presented to the court." Raine's jaw clenched as the demon continued. "This is an extraordinary honor, but there is certain etiquette you must adhere to. Although the Goddess al-lows you great leeway in her private chambers," Faen paused, and his tone indicated he disapproved of this latitude. "You must not engage in such behavior in open court."

Faen again fluttered the scroll in her face, and Raine was on the verge of snatching it from him. He began reading aloud.

"You will walk three steps behind the Goddess, never at her side. You will not speak to her, unless spoken to. You will not eat or drink in her presence. You will not make eye contact with her, but will keep your eyes downcast at all times. You will bow when others bow, you will kneel when others kneel. You will not under any circumstances touch her. And you will not sit in her presence, but remain standing, for no one sits in the presence of the Goddess."

Faen particularly emphasized this, for Raine sat in the presence of the Goddess all the time. It had not occurred to her that no one else did.

"Do you understand these rules of the court?"

Raine ignored him, and he shoved the scroll in her face to where it almost touched her nose. In a blindingly fast move, she snatched the parchment from his hand and threw it with unerring accuracy across the room into the fireplace, where it burst into flames. Faen was stunned at the speed and violence of the move, and more stunned when she leaned down and stared into his face with ice blue eyes.

"I'm going to enjoy killing you."

The demon was infuriated, but also a little afraid, which made him even more angry. It was easy to forget that Hel's Arlanian sex toy was also Scinterian.

At that moment, Hel entered the room and all grew quiet. She stopped abruptly at the sight of Raine, silently contemplating what was before her. And Feray felt an immense pride, for the look on the face of her Mistress told her that she and the handmaidens had done well.

Hel sensed Feray's pride, as well as Faen's discomfiture, the latter which merely entertained her. She also sensed the Arlanian's unwillingness to participate in her public display in the court. But as always, the willingness or unwillingness of her captive was irrelevant to her.

"Come," Hel said, "it is time."

A strange, dark overture began, the music drifting up from below the balcony. The music rose in volume as Hel stepped out onto the terrace to greet her subjects. Feray gestured for Raine to follow her, and as soon as her back was turned, Faen took the opportunity to shove her from behind. She stumbled, glaring at him, but followed Feray.

All bowed before the Queen of the Underworld, and the fanfare turned to crescendo as she started down the steps. Raine stood on the terrace, frozen in place as all eyes turned towards her. A sea of faces, some beautiful, some hideous, some handsome, some demonic, floated before her. Their expressions were leering, curious, entertained, sarcastic, inquisitive, condescending, sneering, probing, and smirking. It was not their expressions which caused Raine to freeze, but rather the wave of lust that struck her like a physical blow. She had suffered the unwanted attentions of others her entire life, but she had never felt the covetousness and desire that washed over her now. She felt unclean as the gazes stripped her, imagined her naked, fantasized what the Goddess did to her every night, or better yet, what they would do if given the chance. Their hunger was like something alive.

Feray glanced to the mortal with concern. It would not look well if they had to drag the Arlanian down the steps; the Goddess would be furious. Even Faen was growing tense. As much as he would have enjoyed shoving this whelp headlong down the staircase, his Mistress would have him flayed alive if this did not go according to plan.

Raine felt two things that brought her peace. The first was that she became very cold, which reminded her that she was still pure amongst pure evil. The second was the welcome presence of her blue and gold markings, the scars that rose on her forearms, biceps, back and shoulders, invisible beneath her clothes, but a welcome reminder that she was not just Arlanian, but Scinterian as well. Half of each, yet fully both, her eyes calmed to a neutral blue, she squared her shoulders, and without further hesitation, began walking down the steps, her head held high. And as she passed the throngs of demons, demi-gods, and magical creatures who fantasized about raping her, she fantasized about killing them. And those nearest her became aware of the disconnect between her vision and theirs, and with a growing discomfort, stepped back from the lethal demeanor that suggested her vision held the more probable outcome.

Hel started up the steps to her throne, her robes flowing behind her, and Raine followed, accompanied by Feray. When they reached the top, Hel turned and stood in front of the throne, and Feray motioned that Raine was to stand off to her left. Raine obeyed the direction and turned to face the assembly. The wave of lust again assaulted her.

The Goddess knew that all attention was on her and her companion.

When she spoke, she gave a quiet command to Raine.

"You will show them your eyes."

It was too much for Raine. "I will not."

Feray stiffened. No one had heard the defiance except her, but all were waiting for something to happen. The servant thought for sure that Hel would strike the mortal down. Instead, the Goddess spoke calmly, still in low tones, her expression never wavering.

"You will show them your eyes or I will rape you on these steps, and they will see your eyes and so much more."

It was Raine's turn to stiffen because there was no doubt in her mind that Hel would carry out her threat. She had no options other than to expose herself and become even more vulnerable than she already was.

The entire assembly gasped with pleasure at the revelation of the violet eyes. A pleased murmur went through the crowd and there was much quiet, ribald, conversation. Their stares were so overt they might as well have been masturbating at the sight of the Arlanian, and Raine thought she saw some reach to touch themselves. Although she tried to maintain her pride, her cheeks flushed with shame as she lowered her head in humiliation. It was bad enough to be paraded through the court as Hel's sex slave, now she felt an object of ridicule.

And then Hel did the strangest thing. She gazed out at her assembly with a degree of disdain, then reached down and placed her fingers beneath Raine's chin. She very gently, but firmly, guided her head upward so that Raine was forced to look at her, and then she bent down and kissed her ever-so-softly.

The court grew silent. Hel drew back, enjoying both the confused look on the Arlanian's face and the eyes that were now so violet they were nearly black. She released her, then settled onto her throne smoothing her robes. She glanced out at the assembly, then gestured with her hand to the bench at her side.

"You will sit down."

Raine did not at first comply. She just stood there, looking at Hel in confusion, entirely uncertain as to what she should do. Then, very slowly, her eyes never leaving the Goddess, she sat down. Given Faen's melodramatic instructions earlier, she was surprised she did not explode on contact with the bench.

Hel gestured to Feray and the handmaiden brought her a glass of wine. Hel gave her a meaningful glance, and Feray understood completely, although she had already grasped the message of the Goddess. She approached Raine and offered her a glass as well, and Raine took the offering, too stunned and confused to contemplate if she even wanted it. She just took it and held it in her hands. Feray gave her a brief bow, the open sign of respect so muddling her thoughts she gave up trying to make sense of the situation.

But Feray had made perfect sense of the situation. The Goddess had clearly communicated a message to all present. The kiss had been utterly possessive, declaring her absolute ownership of the being at her side: this was one that Hel would not share, nor allow to be humiliated. And her subsequent actions were perhaps even more significant. By allowing Raine, in fact commanding her, to sit and drink in her presence, Hel had just elevated the mortal above every other creature in the Underworld.

Raine remembered little of the events of the court. Hel sat in judgment of people, decided some disputes, and issued several edicts. Many sought to curry favor, and all acted with the same fearful reverence before the Goddess. They still cast longing, even lustful glances at the Arlanian, but they did so with a degree of discretion that had been lacking before.

Hel glanced to Raine, noting that she still held the goblet of wine, untouched.

"Drink."

Raine looked down at the glass of wine numbly, as if she had forgotten about it. She lifted the goblet to her lips and took a sip. The wine was exquisite, but its effect was immediate. Raine's vision blurred, then refocused, and she felt a little light-headed. Feray moved to take the glass from her, which she was on the verge of spilling, and Raine tried to clear her head. Most alcohol did not affect her at all, but that made her feel inebriated from one sip.

Hel smiled, for the wine of the gods would kill a normal mortal. She had suspected it would do no such thing with this one. And after watching those lips touch the glass and the wine, observing the unconsciously sensual gestures of the creature next to her, Hel was no longer that interested in the court in front of her. The Arlanian had already been bewildered by events; now her confusion was magnified by the spirits she had just consumed. Hel had every intention of taking advantage of that befuddled state in her bed, preferably as soon as possible.

Feray caught the glance of her Mistress and moved to Raine's side, indicating she should stand. Raine did so, swaying slightly and catching herself. She took a deep breath, willing some self-control. Hel stood and all in the court kneeled before her. According to Faen's instructions, Raine knew she should be kneeling, but she was afraid she might not stay upright if she went to her knees. The Goddess saved her from her uncertainty and held out her hand to Raine. After staring at the appendage for a moment, Raine took it, holding it in the position of escort. And since she had already violated every one of the Faen's rules of etiquette, she escorted the Goddess from the room, walking at her side.

They did not have to proceed through the throne room again. There was a door behind Hel's throne, one that led through a hallway that circled back up to her chambers, and Raine saw the other side of the immoveable door, one that Hel opened with a wave of her hand. Feray followed them in, but then dismissed herself without direction, for truly she had ceased to exist in the eyes of the Goddess.

Hel was extraordinarily pleased with the day in court. What was routine, mundane, even insufferable, was almost pleasant with the Arlanian at her side. And even unknowingly and unwillingly, the mortal had acted with perfection. Raine's current pliability only increased Hel's pleasure, and she undressed her in an unhurried manner and guided her to the bed. Then, determined to take advantage of her relaxed state, the Goddess of the Underworld spent several hours very gently sodomizing her captive lover, bringing her to exquisite release before she herself released on top of her.

Raine awoke many hours later, tangled with the Goddess. Her thoughts were still muddled, perhaps the lingering effects of the wine. And she was exhausted. Just lying skin-to-skin with the Goddess was draining, although, thankfully, that which made her so cold also warmed her. Hel's evil was freezing, but her hot-blooded nature made her skin very warm. Raine shifted and the Goddess reached out in her sleep to wrap her arm around Raine's waist.

Sleep was overtaking Raine once more, but one thought kept circling as she reviewed the events in court. The way Hel treated her was confusing, and more than a little alarming. Raine understood none of the machinations of the court. But the deference with which she was treated felt dangerous, and Raine had the uneasy suspicion it might lead to a worse outcome than had Hel raped her on the steps.

Chapter 9

Maeva signed the parchment with her graceful scrawl, then pushed the pile of paperwork to the side. Although she was much preoccupied these days, the Alfar Republic would not run itself, and as Directorate of the High Council, she could not afford to give in to distraction. But, she admitted to herself, sometimes a break was needed.

"I will return shortly, Melwen," she said, and her trusted assistant nodded, sorting through the remaining paperwork.

The tall, lovely elven woman passed through the archways of the citadel, her almond shaped eyes unfocused as she was lost in thought. The Alfar guards, formidable in their green and gold armor, snapped to attention as she passed, but she barely acknowledged them. Her robes flowed behind her, and the intricate braids in her long hair swayed with her graceful motion. She came to the library, where her brother Feyden and his companions were hard at work. She took a moment to examine his fair features, a masculine version of her own.

"And how goes your task?" Maeva asked him.

"It goes well," Feyden said, indicating the enormous map that was laid on the table in front of them. The scribe who had completed the drawing was a skilled artist, for not only was the map accurate, it was beautiful in a horrible kind of way. Maeva examined the rendition of the Gates of the Underworld, the red and black courtyard, and the other features that the scribe had recreated in detail.

"It is accurate in scale," Feyden said, "or at least as much as we can remember. Dagna's recollection is extraordinary."

"A necessity for a bard," Dagna said, shrugging off the compliment.

"Don't sell yourself short, lass," Lorifal said. "Dwarves have near-perfect recall, and you're putting me to shame."

"And here," Maeva said, still examining the map and tapping it with her finger. "Nothing is known beyond this point here?"

She was indicating the Gates of the Underworld, the true gates at the far end of the red and black courtyard.

"That's correct," Feyden said. "That's where Raine killed the Ancient Dragon, Ragnar, and where Talan destroyed the Scales of Light and Dark so she could shut the gates."

"Hmm," Maeva said. "So it could be hundreds of leagues from that point to the actual Underworld. Or even farther."

"Yes," Feyden said grimly. "We have no idea what is beyond the gates. Our rescue mission could stop right there."

If it even got that far, Maeva thought to herself. Somehow they had to get more information on what was beyond those gates.

"I'm going to go see how Kiren is doing. Maybe she can find something."

Kiren was in the adjacent wing of the library, her small figure dwarfed by the towers of books she had stacked all around her. As she had with her brother, Maeva stopped for a moment to take in the sight of her lover. The raven hair was lustrous in the soft light, her blue eyes glowing like sapphires as Kiren pored over the ancient tomes. She chewed her lower lip, an unconscious gesture that caused desire to flare up in the Directorate.

"And how goes your translation?"

Kiren looked up, breaking into a smile that warmed the icy elven leader as nothing else could.

"I have found something," she said excitedly, then frowned. "Well, a little something. It's not much, but more than we have had before."

Maeva took a position behind Kiren so she could look over her shoulder. Kiren pointed to the primary scroll in front of her. It was old, written in a language that pre-dated even the ancient tongue. Most of it had been translated, but the final line had remained obscure.

"The Dragon's Lover," Kiren said, tracing the graceful markings, "felled by the closest of allies, carries into death without dying, that which saves all worlds."

Kiren's finger moved down to the final markings on the paper. "Some of these words are easier than others. The first one was the easiest. A simple connecting word, a conjunction. I think it means 'and.'" Her finger moved across the markings. "This phrase in the middle seemed connected to the verb 'to be' in the ancient tongue, although it appeared twice with minor variation, and I think it due to a change in tense. I'm fairly certain it reads 'it is to be.'"

"It is to be?" Maeva asked. "What does that mean?"

"Without context, it means nothing," Kiren said. "But that gave me a clue to the second word, which seemed similar to the first line, 'the Dragon's Lover' in that it seems to refer to the same thing, in a general sense, and is also possessive. I think the translation is 'whose,' referring to the Dragon's Lover."

"And whose 'blank' it is to be?"

"Yes," Kiren said enthusiastically, "which narrowed down what the third word could be. And I found this," she said, dragging a scroll from a disorderly pile, "which gave me a clue. This is an allegory involving judgment, and has a word in it that we translate as 'luck' or 'chance.' But that meaning has changed much over time. If you trace its derivation and follow the etymology backwards, it originally meant something closer to 'fate' or 'destiny.'"

"I see," Maeva said, impressed with her young lover's intelligence.

"So thus far," Kiren summarized, "the prophecy reads: 'The Dragon's Lover, felled by the closest of allies, carries into death without dying, that which saves all worlds, and whose destiny it is to be....'"

Hearing Kiren recite the prophecy in its known entirety made the import of her words sink it. This final line declared Raine's fate.

"Do you have any idea what the remainder of the line says?"

"Not yet," Kiren said, frowning. "It appears to be some type of title, but I've found nothing that has given me any insight. I will keep working."

Maeva leaned down and kissed Kiren's raven hair. "You have made more progress than all the elven scholars combined. You will figure it out."

Maeva started to leave, then remembered why she had come into the room in the first place.

"Oh, Feyden and the others are still hard at work creating maps of their journey to the Underworld. But they never went past Hel's Gate. If you find anything in your studies that would shed light on what lies beyond, they would appreciate your help."

Kiren nodded, mentally adding it to her list of things to do, then returned to the symbols that so perplexed her.

Chapter 10

The Tree of Death loomed ominously over the far side of the garden, still bleeding its golden yellow sap. Raine stood beneath it, drawn to its gloomy, misshapen outline for reasons she couldn't quite fathom. It seemed to pulse and glow with an inner light, but the light did not warm or illuminate, merely seemed to twist about inside as if trying to escape the dark confines of its bark prison.

Thoughts crept into Raine's mind, thoughts she had steadfastly pushed away the entire time she had been in the Underworld. She would not taint those thoughts or memories with any association with this place. But still, they seemed stronger, insistent, when standing before this tree. And although she fought to suppress them, perhaps that is what drew her to the spot day-after-day.

"You are thinking of her."

Raine jumped, startled by the proximity of the Goddess, who was suddenly right next to her. She shivered from cold, and from the very dangerous tone in Hel's voice. She decided to say nothing.

But Raine did not have to say anything. The Goddess had seen the deep violet of her eyes as she contemplated the Tree of Death, and knew what had generated the color.

"Strange," the Goddess said, "that you have not once asked about her the entire time you have been here. Or truly, about any of your friends at all."

Raine clenched her jaw, but still said nothing. She would not give

Hel the satisfaction of making her beg for information. And there was no way the conversation would play out in any beneficial way for her, which is why she hadn't asked. She knew that Weynild was alive, and Skye as well. Beyond that, she knew nothing.

Her silence angered Hel even further.

"You will prepare for court," Hel said coldly, turning about with a whirl of her cloak.

They entered the throne room, much as before, but this time when Hel sat, she did not give Raine permission to sit. Faen's red eyes glittered with glee, for he could tell his Mistress was very angry at the mortal, and that meant it would be a good day in court. Feray merely stood circumspectly in the shadows.

Raine stood stiffly at Hel's side, gazing out at the assembly with unseeing eyes. She felt numb, cold, particularly lifeless at the moment. She cared nothing for the proceedings, although she did note that Hel was merciless today. She might have felt compassion for the judged were they not so wholly beyond redemption.

Even so, Raine grew uneasy when one particular man was brought forth in chains. He appeared somewhat human, but Raine did not think that he was, rather perhaps a demi-god or some other magical creature. He was afraid, shaking, and although his crime was horrendous, something to do with some sort of sexual crime, Raine almost felt pity for him. The jeers and catcalls of the crowd were loud, louder than they had been for any of the damned, and the crowd seemed excited by the nature of his crime.

And then Raine understood why. The Membrane, that horrible amalgam of limbs and sexual parts, floated in from the back of the enormous room. The crowd cheered, but also stayed clear of the horrific creature as it glided in to do its Mistress' bidding. Hel watched impassively as the man tried to flee, straining against his chains, then fell to the ground, whimpering.

Raine took an inadvertent step back, feeling the hard edge of the bench against the back of her knees. Her movement caught Hel's eye, who glanced at her, then returned her attention to the punishment unfolding.

Feray looked on with the same impassivity of her Mistress, while Faen nearly bounced around in delight.

The Membrane settled over the man and Raine had to turn away. She could not shut out the man's screams, or the disgusting sucking noises the creature made as it did whatever it was doing. Hel viewed the proceedings with little interest, but turned to her captive with idle curiosity. Many Arlanians were unwillingly excited even by acts that disgusted them, as long as the acts were sexual in nature. Raine, however, showed no such response as her eyes were so pale a blue they were almost gray. For some reason, this pleased Hel.

Raine breathed out, and the arm of Hel's throne was encased in ice, a phenomenon Hel examined with interest. Raine tried to look anywhere but at the scene in front of her, but there was no safe place for her eyes to rest. The crowd swam before her eyes, their leering, jeering features distorted. The screams and yells and cheers sounded as if she were underwater. Faen's awful expression stretched out to an exaggerated length, mocking her. She sought desperately to block out everything around her, but the rising pain in her body was making it hard to focus.

Hel's attention was now entirely on Raine. The mortal was shivering uncontrollably as she brought a shaking hand to her chest, rubbing it as if in pain. Her breathing was shallow and those beautiful lips were turning blue. She swayed as if she were about to fall, clearly on the verge of collapse. Her knees buckled, and she would have fallen to the stone floor had not Hel reached out and hooked a finger in the sash about her waist. With merely a tug, the Goddess shifted Raine's weight so that when she fell, she did not plummet to the ground but rather collapsed on top of her, and Hel caught her easily in her arms.

Raine stared up at the Goddess who held her. The emerald eyes were filled with an amused sarcasm at her captive's undignified position. Indeed, Hel held her much as one would hold a child, although the embrace was far more controlling than tender. The Goddess did not speak, for she did not need to. And for Raine, the indignity of the position was nothing; she just wanted to be away from the scene in front of her. She wanted to block out the horrible sounds, to hide from the terrible acts, to erase the memory of the entire event. And so great was her despair, she turned and buried her face in the breasts of the Goddess in an attempt to escape what was in front of her.

"Mmm," Hel said, inordinately pleased with the act, involuntary or not. A flush of color returned to the Arlanian's cheeks as she was warmed by the skin she pressed against. Her eyes were tightly closed, her body still tense as it strained to get as far away as possible from the evil and carnality below her.

The sight of the Arlanian collapsing, and the far more improbable sight of the Goddess holding her, now garnered as much attention as the rapacious assault of the Membrane. The cheers and jeers diminished, which made the man's screams all the louder, causing Raine to flinch as if struck.

Hel merely sighed, and with a sweep of her arm, covered Raine completely with her cloak. And this was no ordinary cloak, for it instantly isolated Raine from all else, blocking out all sight, sound, and sensation, so that she was left in silence and warmth, pressed up against the Goddess in darkness and quiet. Hel could feel the tension drain from the Arlanian's body as she clutched at the cloth of her gown.

Faen observed the action in disbelief and fury, the latter he tempered abruptly when his Mistress cast her glance his way. Feray, on the other hand, had observed the entire exchange, and was not certain if her Mistress' actions were due to pragmatism, pity, or possessiveness. In the end, she concluded it was probably a combination of all three, with the first and last holding sway, and the middle having the least influence of all.

Hel did not interrupt the proceedings of her court, rather continued them with the Arlanian asleep on her lap beneath her cloak. This at first attracted much interest and whispered conversation. But the interest gradually diminished, and the action that at first was extraordinary now felt merely fitting. The Goddess stroked the head of her unconscious captive as one would stroke a favored pet. And the submissive, even defeated position of the Arlanian brought pleasure to all as they contemplated what the Goddess would do with her helpless companion once the day was through.

Chapter 11

The Queen of the Ha'kan sat with her High Priestess on the terrace overlooking her castle courtyard. They sipped their tea, talking softly. A somber mood had fallen upon the Ha'kan as a whole, much like the years they had battled the Tavinter. Although day-to-day life was largely the same, the fate of Raine and Talan, their staunchest allies and dearest friends, weighed heavily on them.

Still, there were bright spots in the dark days, and one of these causes for joy was approaching them. Lifa, the future High Priestess, flowed towards them, the child she carried within just beginning to show. Astrid rose and kissed her future successor on the forehead.

"And how are you feeling today, my love?"

Lifa was quietly radiant as she took the Queen's proffered hand. "I feel fine, thank you. Kara gives me a check-up every morning, so I assure you my health is good."

Lifa settled onto the cushioned bench next to Astrid and accepted a cup of tea. "And I am constantly surrounded by Dallan, Rika, and all my priestesses, even more so than usual."

"And that one?" Astrid asked, nodding to a solitary figure leaning against the balcony railing on the adjacent terrace.

"Especially that one," Lifa said, "by my own demand."

The three women watched Skye for a moment, who seemed absorbed in her own thoughts.

"The Tavinter like to retreat when they are saddened," Lifa said, "and so we give her space. But none of us will allow her to sleep alone."

"That's good," Astrid said, "and I know that Senta and Gimle have both taken Skye to their beds of late, for the same reason. They have reported that she expresses her grief much like we do."

It was a statement with a hint of a question, a question which Lifa answered.

"That is so. She is melancholy, but as passionate in bed as always."

"Good," Astrid said again. She cocked her head to one side. "What is she looking at?"

Skye was no longer leaning against the balcony but standing upright, and she was no longer lost in thought, but staring intently off into the distance. A series of flashing lights were visible from far away. The message was not for Skye, but rather for the Tavinter that stood at the message station on the city gates of the Ha'kan capital, but Skye could read it. She began walking across the bridge that joined the two terraces, unhurried, but at a good pace.

"Your Majesty," Skye said, bowing formally. "High Priestess." She reached out and took Lifa's hand, simply squeezing it as a greeting.

"Good morning, Skye," Halla said warmly. "Is there a message from your scouts?"

"Yes," Skye said, "there are two dragons on the way. But they are flying very fast and very high, and they have not been identified."

"Where are they now?" the Queen asked, concerned.

"The message was relayed from the border, but at their speed, they will be here soon."

"Skye," Halla said, "you should find Senta. We should prepare—"

"There is no need," Idonea said, having made her way across the bridge from the adjacent terrace. "One of the dragons is my brother."

The Queen was visibly relieved. "Drakar? That is wonderful news. And the other?"

"I don't know," Idonea said. "But I can feel my brother's presence, so I know it's him."

"Please have a cup of tea while we wait for him."

Idonea accepted the invitation, as did Skye, and the five women sat awaiting the dragons' arrival.

"And how are you feeling, Idonea?" Astrid asked gently. The dark-haired mage was generally filled with a reckless exuberance. The mature, focused intensity she exhibited now was starkly different from her usual manner.

"I am well, High Priestess, thank you."

"You know you are welcome to avail yourself of the services of our Ministry," Astrid said delicately.

Idonea started to decline the invitation, then stopped. She had studiously avoided her normal flirtatious behavior, concentrating on her training. But a little extracurricular activity might relieve some pressure, especially one requiring no emotional investment. And if it felt like she was abdicating her responsibility, she assuaged herself with the thought that her mother, whose lust was legendary even for a dragon, would only approve.

Astrid could see Idonea waver, so she gently pushed her over the edge. "And really, all of the Priestess caste would be available to you."

Skye choked on her tea while a smile played about the lips of the Ha'kan Queen. Lifa did not hide her smile at all; the offer from her mentor was so skillfully inserted into the conversation it prompted nothing but admiration.

Idonea shifted in her seat. She was usually the aggressor with both men and women, and as such, unused to being seduced. It was a novel experience for her. The sultry elegance of the High Priestess was both powerful and magnetic, and Idonea inwardly reiterated her opinion that the non-magical Ha'kan were magical in their own way.

"I think I would like that very much, High Priestess," Idonea said, "I have a full day, but my evening is free." She then leaned forward and slapped Skye on the back before she choked to death.

"I think I see the dragons," Halla said.

The women stood as one and Skye regained her composure enough to use her very acute eyesight.

"The second dragon is big," Skye said, "and blue."

Hope stirred in Idonea. "He has found Kylan."

Talan had been on her way to secure the assistance of her kind when Hel had appeared before Raine on the battlefield. Sensing the danger to her beloved, the Ancient Dragon sought to pass through Nifelheim to rescue her. Instead, she had been ambushed, and Raine had sacrificed herself in an attempt to rescue Talan, and both had disappeared. But no one knew what had become of the dragons that were supposed to come to their aid in the battle that never happened.

Idonea did not possess Skye's eyesight, but she could feel the dark magic in the one approaching, magic exceeded only by that of her mother. The dragons grew larger and became distinct. Drakar's ebony wings and sleek body were prominent against the pale blue sky. Kylan glittered silvery in the light, her massive frame moving with the particular grace of the Ancient ones. They let out distinct roars as they circled the capital city, then dove downward towards the terrace. Drakar arrived first, pulling up sharply and coming into a dramatic landing whereas Kylan took a more leisurely ascent, landing with the gentlest of earthquakes. Massive talons scraped against the stone and the heavy plating made a grating sound as the dragon scales scraped against one another. A flash of red light, followed by a flash of silver, blinded the women standing on the terrace, and the two dragons disappeared. A darkly handsome man dressed in black stepped forward. His well-trimmed mustache and dashing goatee offset flashing black eyes, and he bore more than a passing resemblance to Idonea. He held his hand out to his raven-haired companion, silver streaking her hair, as beautiful and magnificent in human form as she was in dragon. Although normally garbed in a blue gown, today she wore dragon-scale armor, and much like Talan's, it was the same color in both her manifestations. Both Kylan and Drakar were known for deviltry and good humor, and neither had a trace of those emotions on their faces today. Fatigue clouded Kylan's lovely features, and it was apparent Drakar held his hand out as much for support as from simple chivalry. Idonea quickened her step.

"Kylan!" she said as she approached, unable to hide the tremor in her voice. Kylan took one look at the somber young woman, saw the tears threatening to spill out of her eyes, and held out her arms.

"Oh, come here, my love."

Idonea buried her head against Kylan's shoulder, welcoming the strong, maternal embrace of the Ancient Dragon. Drakar's throat ached as a lump formed. Idonea had shown little emotion since their mother had been taken, but she had reacted exactly as he had upon first sight of Kylan. Kylan was Talan's most trusted ally amongst dragonkind, and so very much like their mother in many ways.

Idonea leaned back and brushed angrily at her tears. "You're injured."

"A scratch," Kylan said dismissively. "And I've nearly slept it off these weeks. We were ambushed by Volva's forces when we were trying to reach the battlefield."

Idonea nodded. "Volva was with the Hyr'rok'kin in the Empty Land, but she was accompanied by only a handful of lesser dragons."

"Yes, all others attacked us in a most cowardly manner." The steel in her voice matched that in her eyes. "They paid for it with their annihilation. But your mother," Kylan herself had to pause from her emotion, "your mother felt the arrival of the Goddess and used the fade bracelet, and that was the last I saw of her."

"We never saw her again, either," Idonea said. "I can only guess that Hel laid a trap for her in Nifelheim, and that was why Raine dove into that portal."

Kylan sighed. "And so she trapped them both."

"Raine is still alive," Skye said, having approached with the others. "I am connected to her, and I can still feel the connection."

Kylan considered these words, and glanced to Idonea, seeing that she, too, understood the ramifications. Talan and her Scinterian were bound to one another, so if Raine was alive, that meant Talan was alive as well. But who knew under what conditions?

"Kylan," the Queen said gently, "we have many healers, and my First Scholar is very skilled. What can we do to help you with your injuries?"

"Thank you, your Majesty, but I believe the one who can help me the most is living in your garden. Magical creatures often require magical solutions."

"Ah," Halla said in understanding, "Y'arren and Elyara are both here."

"I will take you to them," Idonea said. "So I will see you around seven this evening?" Idonea asked, addressing the High Priestess.

"I look forward to it," Astrid said.

For once, Drakar felt no jealousy regarding his sister. She had been so melancholy; it might do her some good. The Divine knew he had been plowing everything that moved.

The Ancient Dragon walked off arm-in-arm with the children of her liege, and Kylan's voice drifted back to them as she addressed Idonea.

"The High Priestess herself? Your mother would be so proud."

Chapter 12

The ball of light floated leisurely towards its target as Y'arren watched closely. Idonea stood with her arms crossed, also observing the benign-looking object float across the courtyard. Their vigilance seemed out of proportion to the harmless looking spell, but this ball of light was no ordinary magical creation. It was pure energy, a manifestation of unadulterated light magic, as dangerous as anything that dark magic could produce.

"Now bring it to a stop," Y'arren instructed.

Skye took a deep breath, manipulated her hands from a distance, and the orb slowed, then stopped, hovering in front of the target.

Idonea nodded in approval. This was a great advancement. Skye had been able to produce the energy before, but had been unable to control it in any way. Once she had started it on a trajectory, it continued indefinitely in a straight line path, at the same speed, in the same direction, leisurely destroying everything in its path. She had nearly unleashed disaster on the castle as a previous attempt began an unstoppable excursion through the palace, and only Raine's presence and her immunity to magic had averted that catastrophe. Idonea, whose skill with light magic was considerable for one whose blood was filled with dark magic, had been able to teach Skye the spell, but unable to teach her how to control it. The ancient elven seer, filled with the power of the natural world, had filled that gap in Skye's education.

"Now draw it back to you," Y'arren directed.

Skye took another deep breath, moved her hands in a wide arc, and slowly the ball began floating back towards her. A sheen of sweat gathered on her forehead, perhaps from concentration, or perhaps from the knowledge that the orb would burn a hole right through her if she failed to stop it. But she raised her hand as the ball neared, it hiccuped slightly in its motion, slowed, then came to a complete stop. The light bathed her features in a warm glow as it hovered before her.

"Now dismiss it," Y'arren said.

Skye slowly lowered both hands, and the ball of light winked out.

Only then did Idonea release her breath. The spell that Skye was utilizing was extremely powerful, and made even more so by the fact that Skye used only light magic. Most mages were proficient in one or the other, but even those who specialized in light magic still used dark magic on occasion. Skye had never done so, and her gift possessed a purity that was both potent and dangerous. When she had used this spell before, she had been unable to dismiss the orb, and there were some she had created in battle that were conceivably still floating across the realm.

Y'arren put her hand on Skye's shoulder, and Skye welcomed the affectionate gesture. Y'arren exuded warmth and love, even in the worst of times, and her quiet confidence was a blessing beyond measure.

"Isleif would be proud of you," Y'arren said.

The mention of her great-grandfather caused a slight ache in her chest, but the pain was lessening with time. Isleif had passed away peacefully in his sleep, and her grief for him followed a normal progression. But Raine had been wrenched violently from their world, and the anguish of that loss was undiminished. Only constant practice seemed to take away that sting.

"Thank you," Skye said, "I couldn't do this without your help."

"You're tired," Idonea observed, "why don't you go play on the archery range or something?"

"That sounds like a good idea," Skye said, and waved goodbye to Elyara who sat near the opening of her tent.

"I would advise most to rest after such exertion," Y'arren said, watching the young woman walk away, "but that one needs activity right now."

"Archery is practically rest for Skye, she does it so effortlessly. Besides," Idonea said, tilting her head to the side, "I think she's about to get quite a bit of activity."

Y'arren nodded. She, too, had felt the presence of the one to whom Idonea referred. And in her wise, neutral way, she neither approved nor disapproved of the choices the Tavinter had made, simply hoped they would serve their purpose.

"Ah, here she is," Rika exclaimed, happy to see Skye approaching. The future First General brushed short brown hair from her eyes, her handsome features made even more appealing by her grin. Dallan, too, was glad to see Skye, and the dark eyes of the Ha'kan Princess flashed with pleasure.

"Your bow is over here," Dallan called out, having saved the lane next to them in case Skye made an appearance.

"Thank you," Skye said, picking up the weapon from the rack. She ran her fingers over the risers, appreciating the smooth curves and lines of her bow. The Tavinter were not a particularly large people and relied on stealth instead of brute strength. Because of that, they were exceptional archers, and none were as skilled as their young leader. The Tavinter bow was a cross between a long bow and a short bow, a compromise that would have reduced its effectiveness with less skilled archers. But the Tavinter exploited the design, able to fire as far and forcefully as with a long bow, yet nearly as quickly as with a short bow. Skye wasted no time in displaying such an ability, sending arrow after arrow down range with jaw-dropping accuracy. Rika grinned again, and Dallan just shook her head and resumed her training.

Although completely focused, Skye became aware of someone standing near her. She glanced to her right to observe the incongruous sight of a stunning woman dressed in an elaborate red gown standing on the muddy training field. The ruby color of the dress offset her long white hair and pale, smooth skin, and Skye's eyes were drawn to the cleavage pushed upwards by the tight bodice. She did not miss a beat, but continued to fire down range even with the distraction, sometimes not even looking at her target.

"Hard to believe, with all your magical skill, you still play with these toys."

Skye swiveled her shoulders and fired an arrow directly at the woman, which should have impaled her through the heart. But it did not, as it was stopped in mid-air inches from those beautiful breasts.

"And what is that for?" Ingrid said, brushing the arrow away as if it were a pesky fly.

"You're late," Skye said. She had known the arrow would not touch Ingrid, for the sorceress possessed power rivaled only by that of Idonea.

"I believe I'm early," Ingrid said, glancing up at the sun. "The full moon will not rise for another few hours."

Skye fired another volley of arrows down range. "Where were you last month?"

Ingrid was silent. The Tavinter still exasperated her with her unpredictability. She had thought the girl utterly predictable, and truly she had been most of her life as Ingrid had hunted her as prey, the consequence of a life-long blood feud between her and Isleif. But the girl had surprised Ingrid by offering her a truce, promising to spend every full moon with her, and allowing her to do whatever she wished to her during that interval.

"I thought," the sorceress said, "it might be appropriate to give you some time to grieve."

This statement finally brought Skye's endless barrage of arrows to a halt. She looked over at Ingrid, a blackly humorous look on her face. This woman had kidnapped her, tortured her, taken away her memory, threatened her life, threatened her friends, kept her as a sexual toy, and regularly drank her blood to retain her youthful appearance. She did all of this in the name of revenge against the man whom she was now professing to give Skye the time to grieve. Even Ingrid seemed to sense the absurdity in this statement.

"Well," Ingrid said, "believe what you will. But it is the truth."

"The truth is," Skye said, notching another arrow, "I would have enjoyed the company."

This was another thing that always put the sorceress off-balance. The girl was remarkably honest, a characteristic that normally she could exploit, but with the girl, only seemed to place her at a disadvantage.

"Is everything all right?" Rika called out across the field to Skye. The appearance of the sorceress had attracted enormous attention from the surrounding Ha'kan, partially because she was a known enemy, and partially because her breasts were almost impossible to look away from.

"Mind your business, Ha'kan," Ingrid said irritably, and Rika only grinned.

"I'm fine," Skye said. She at last set her bow to the side and turned her full attention to the sorceress. Her eyes swept the curvaceous figure with an appreciation she did not bother to hide. A flush of color appeared on that pale skin.

"Well," Ingrid said coolly, "perhaps we can make up for last month's absence by starting early."

Skye took her by the hand.

"That would be acceptable."

Skye was tied spread-eagled to the bed, her restraints created by some infernal magic she had never seen before. Ingrid had taken quite an interest in the Ha'kan sexual toys, and was gifted in creating magical equivalents to them. When Skye had made the mistake of mentioning Kara, the future First Scholar who was known for wild sexual exploration, Ingrid determined to meet her. Skye was grateful that this consultation had yet to take place, for Kara had created some of the most inventive sexual gadgets ever known. Skye could not imagine their magical equivalent.

She was, however, enjoying the magical equivalent of one of those devices right now, one that happened to have been sitting around. And Ingrid's adoption of it was inspired, for it feathered the backside, penetrated deep on the inside, and allowed Ingrid's mouth the freedom to travel where it willed. And it traveled the extent of Skye's body, taking an extended amount of time until it settled between her legs and brought Skye to her first climax.

Ingrid, surprisingly, was not a selfish lover. Self-centered in all her other pursuits, she took great pleasure in bringing Skye to orgasm. Perhaps it was because it gave her a sense of control; she did enjoy utterly dominating the young woman. Or perhaps it was because it heightened her own sexual pleasure. But Ingrid always ensured that Skye was satisfied.

That was not to say she deferred her own gratification. No sooner had Skye climaxed, she modified the magical device so that it thrust up inside her, then rode the girl so hard it was a wonder Skye did not break in two.

But Skye was hardy in bed, possessing a stamina that had been refined by years of living with the Ha'kan. And with those lovely, pink-tipped breasts bouncing above her head, those supple hips grinding against her own, it was not long before she climaxed again, carried away by the angry passion of the sorceress.

Chapter 13

There was some sort of celebration planned for Hel's court, that much Raine had figured out. A strange energy hummed and throbbed throughout the underground palace. Servants scurried about with purpose. Arrangements were argued over, procedure was decided, an agenda was set. Food and drink were in abundance, music played quietly from an alcove. There was an air of anticipation.

Raine had also figured out over time that "court" was a title used in multiple meanings. The Goddess of the Underworld did indeed sit in judgment of those who deserved punishment, but the throne room also acted as her royal court, a place for diplomacy and gathering. The celebration planned for the day was in Hel's honor, and Feray took particular care in dressing Raine so that she looked even more stunning than usual. Her pants were black, her shirt and vest a deep royal purple, the same color as that of the trim on Hel's black robes, and also the color of Raine's eyes if they turned. And her eyes did turn when Hel entered, for the Goddess was gorgeous in her dark raiment, a fact that Raine noted with considerable discomfort.

The court awaited the entrance of the Goddess, and many wagers were exchanged prior to her appearance. It had become a maxim amongst the regulars that they could instantly tell the mood of the Goddess by the position of the Arlanian when Hel entered the court. If Hel was in a good mood, Raine walked at her side, holding her hand upright in the position of escort. If Hel was in a foul mood, Raine walked several steps behind, sandwiched between Feray and Faen like a prisoner on her way to execution. Raine was not certain which position she preferred. The latter was humiliating, but the former emphasized the intimacy between them. It did not matter what Raine preferred, however, for it was the will of the Goddess that decided all.

The court breathed easier when the Goddess appeared, for as her Majesty started down the stairs, the Arlanian was at her side. The expression on the face of the Arlanian was blank as she passed all with unseeing eyes, but she maintained her proper position with effortless grace. And when they reached the throne, Hel settled onto the cushioned seat, smoothed her robes, then indicated that Raine was to sit at her side. This brought a few titters in the very back of the immense room, and a few derisive observations that it was better the Arlanian was seated in the event she collapsed into unconsciousness again.

The entertainment began and it ranged from the violently acrobatic to the blatantly sexual. The sexual acts did not interest Raine and her eyes did not vary from the pale blue to which they had stabilized. The swordplay did interest her, and she unconsciously opened and closed her hand with the desire to be holding a weapon. Hel observed the involuntary gesture, and the blue and gold markings that rose on the forearm. Remarkable that the carnality before the mortal was insufficient to bring forth the color in her eyes, but the swordplay brought out the Scinterian in her instantly.

The entertainers finished their exhibition to grand applause. Even Hel deigned a nod of approval, a gesture in importance exceeding the sum total of the boisterous appreciation in the hall. Raine did not respond, and shook her head when Feray offered her a glass of wine. Hel was unmoved by Raine's disinterest, for what came next would surely shake the Arlanian from her lethargy.

The shuffling of the crowd at the bottom of the stairs told Raine that it was time for the presentations, an endless parade of sycophants seeking to curry the favor of the Goddess. But oddly, the crowd was parting for a solo figure who was unexpected by all but Hel. Gasps accompanied his presence, and a frenzy of anticipation attended his path through the enormous hall. Despite the carnival atmosphere his arrival provoked, he was greeted with great respect and given ample room to make his way across the hall. He stopped at the bottom of the stairs, his expression stern and unwavering as Hel looked upon him with amusement.

Raine examined him. He stood head and shoulders over all near him. He was extraordinarily handsome with shoulder length, wavy dark brown hair, dark brown eyes, and a broadly muscular body currently filled with tension. His long eyelashes flicked to Raine as he glanced in her direction, then returned his attention to Hel. His frown did not mar his fine-looking features, rather gave him a brooding intensity that increased his allure. Although Raine had never seen this man before, she knew instantly who he was.

She took a deep breath, steeling herself for the humiliation of having to ask for something that should have been her right. She turned to the Goddess.

"May I go speak with him?"

Hel examined her beautiful captive, pleased with the submission in that simple request. She took Raine's chin in her hand, leaned forward, and gave her the gentlest of kisses. She leaned back, even more pleased at the violet her kiss evoked.

"You may."

Raine stood, straightened her clothing, squared her shoulders, then started down the steps with every pair of eyes in the room upon her. She moved with the lithe, deadly grace that, although always present, seemed to disappear in the shadow of the Goddess. Without Hel's looming presence, however, that lethality became apparent to many in the hall, causing them to look upon her as if seeing her for the very first time. She seemed less a plaything at the moment than a tightly contained being, a trapped animal that was cornered but could explode at any time.

Raine stopped before the man, leaving an appropriate distance between them although in truth, she wanted none. She took a deep breath to steady her voice, to wring from it the deep emotion that was threatening to spill forth.

"I think I like you better in your other form."

"As do I," Fenrir said, "but my sister does not allow it in her realm."

Raine struggled to maintain her demeanor. She carefully considered her words, knowing they were heard by all in the room, and most closely monitored by she who sat on the throne.

"You are well?" Raine asked.

"I am," Fenrir said, "but my children miss you." His voice was controlled, but thick with emotion. "I miss you."

Raine could not respond. The ache in her throat was too acute.

"And how are you?" Fenrir asked.

"As well as can be expected under the circumstances."

The words held a world of meanings, all of which Fenrir understood. It was the diplomatic reply of someone in an impossible situation.

"Good. I had heard report. But I had to see you with my own eyes."

"Thank you for coming."

Their short conversation seemed at an end, and both stood stiffly apart. Finally, Raine turned as if to leave.

"Raine—"

Raine did not even have to look at his face, because his voice held all of their mutual pain. She turned back to him as he pulled her into his arms, embracing her tightly as she buried her face in his chest. The inhabitants of the Underworld gaped in stunned silence as the wolf god clung to the mortal with an anguish that was palpable.

Although Raine would have stayed in that embrace for hours, even their momentary weakness was dangerous. She pulled back from him and he, too, regained his composure.

"I hope to see you again," Raine said.

"I will do everything I can to return," Fenrir said, and Raine turned and started back up the steps.

Hel watched the display of affection with a jaundiced eye. On the one hand, it made her jealous of Raine's love of Fenrir, a love he so obviously returned. On the other hand, it was nice to have her brother beneath her heel once more. These two emotions seemed to cancel one another out, so she was left with little if any response to the exchange. With the Arlanian safely settled at her side once more, she turned her attention to her brother.

Fenrir bowed low, his respect as much to keep Raine safe as from any genuine feeling.

"Thank you for receiving me, your Majesty."

"You are always welcome here, my brother." Hel's hand drifted over to settle possessively on Raine's leg. "We look forward to your return."

Fenrir bowed once more, then made his way back through the hall, his stormy countenance causing the crowd to give him an even wider berth as he sliced through them. He stopped only at the entrance, to where he leaned down to Garmr, whispering a few words to the snarling beast.

"If you even think to touch her," Fenrir said through gritted teeth that were already returning to fangs, "I will rip off your balls and shove them down your throat."

His words were heard by none but the watchdog, but all could hear Garmr whimper as he put his tail between his legs, and backed into a corner.

A hum of speculation followed Fenrir's exit. The murmurs revolved around his startling arrival, the strange and unexpected bond between him and the mortal, and even of Hel's acknowledgement of Fenrir by her use of the term "brother." Proposed theories flew about, all trying to interpret the many-layered meaning of the short visit.

Raine attempted no such interpretation. She sat there even more numb than before, the brief reunion leaving her raw and dazed. She could not fathom Hel's intent on a normal day. If possible, the extraordinary event provided her even less insight.

Hel, however, was rather pleased with how the reunion had unfolded. Although she had said little to her brother, she had communicated to him exactly what she wished him to know.

Chapter 14

The Queen made her way across the garden, accompanied by her First General and First Scholar. Their swift approach was observed by Y'arren's attendants, who disappeared inside the flap of the tent, then reappeared with the elven matriarch. Elyara came out behind her, and Kylan, who had been resting on the cot inside, followed her. Drakar and Idonea sat on a bench not far away from Y'arren's camp, and they, too, observed the determined approach of the Queen. Their curiosity drew them in and they joined Y'arren in waiting for Queen Halla. Dallan and Skye also appeared at a side gate, jogging to an intercept course with the Queen's entourage, and falling in behind them.

"Y'arren," Halla said, slightly out of breath, "a man appeared at the front gate not long ago, asking to see you, and he is being escorted here now."

"A man?" Y'arren asked. "Elven?"

The Queen looked to her First General, who had been at the gates when the man arrived. Senta shook her head.

"I don't think so," Senta said, "he is a man—," she stopped, at a loss for words. "—quite unlike any I've ever seen. But I felt compelled to allow him entrance."

"What does he look like?" Y'arren asked.

"Huge," Senta said, "taller than me. He looks enormously strong, long brown hair, brown eyes, strong white teeth, gloomy and menacing."

Y'arren contemplated this description, then said only "I see."

The group was left with this enigmatic response, but not for long as the Royal Guard escorted the man through the garden. He drew the attention of all. Ha'kan women were rarely attracted to non-Ha'kan, and the male of any species held no interest to them at all. But as this dark creature stalked through their garden, many privately thought that if they were ever to dip their toe in that pool, this would be the specimen with which to do so.

As he approached, Y'arren kneeled down, followed by her attendants. Idonea, Drakar, and even Kylan went to a knee, and the Ha'kan, surprised by the display of reverence and uncertain what was happening, also kneeled.

"That is enough of that," Fenrir growled uncomfortably.

Y'arren rose gracefully to her feet. "You will have to forgive us. It is not every day we are afforded a visit from a god."

This brought gasps from the Ha'kan.

"I dislike this form," Fenrir said, "but I thought it would sooner gain me admission than my preferred visage."

"Queen Halla," Y'arren said, "do you object if Fenrir returns to his natural form?"

"No," the Queen said, regaining her composure, "of course not."

Fenrir did not hesitate, his appearance wavered, grew smoky, then in an instant, he twisted into a gigantic wolf that stood upright on its hind legs. Skye stared in wonder, recognizing the beast she had seen with Raine on their quest through the forest.

"Thank you," Fenrir said. "I can breathe much easier."

"And why have you blessed us with your presence, wolf god?" Y'arren asked

Fenrir brushed distractedly at his silky coat with an enormous paw. "I have been to the Underworld, and I have seen Raine."

"Is she all right?" Skye said, stepping forward.

Fenrir recognized the young Tavinter who had accompanied Raine through the forest, the one who had helped rescue one of his children from poachers.

"In her words, as well as can be expected under the circumstances."

"You spoke to her?" Y'arren said.

"I did. My sister allowed me to enter her realm."

"Your sister?" Gimle began, then caught herself. "That's right, you are

Hel's brother."

"I am," Fenrir said, as if the fact gave him no pleasure. "We have not spoken in ages, but I swallowed my pride in order to see Raine."

Fenrir then described their brief interaction, trying to recall as much detail as possible.

"She was uninjured?" Y'arren asked.

"She does not appear to be harmed in any way, and no one, other than my sister, has the opportunity to harm her, for she is never far from Hel's grasp."

"Did you—?" Idonea began, then stopped. She gathered herself. "Did you see any sign of Talan?"

"I did not see any sign of your mother," Fenrir said with sympathy, "but I was not allowed beyond the throne room."

Kylan frowned and put her arm around Idonea's shoulders. She ached for the dragon's children, and she ached for herself.

"Did you get any sense of Raine's position?" the Queen asked.

"I will not lie to you," Fenrir rumbled, "it is clear that Hel has taken Raine to her bed, and takes enormous pleasure in her as a lover. It is also clear this is against Raine's will, and she submits because she has no choice."

"And because she is Arlanian," Y'arren said, stating what the wolf god did not wish to.

"Yes," Fenrir said, "because she is Arlanian."

Y'arren mulled these words, because this had long been Raine's fear of her fate. Talan had sought for years to prepare her for the possibility, insisting that she feel no guilt or shame if her body responded to the Goddess. Y'arren hoped that the wise words of the dragon had taken hold, or Raine's helpless position was all the worse.

Fenrir's next words only added to Y'arren's unease.

"There is something else," he said, "something about the way Raine is being treated in the Underworld."

"Is she abused?" the Queen asked with concern.

"No," Fenrir said, "I would almost prefer that were the case. But my sister treats Raine in a way I have never seen her treat anyone, with an inexplicable deference, and an absolute demand that others treat her the same way."

Fenrir thought back to the subtle cues he had identified, the little displays of etiquette that most likely meant nothing to Raine, and yet everything to those in Hel's court.

"I don't know what Hel is doing, but I see a great danger in this elevation of Raine, this recognition of her. My sister never does anything without a reason."

The group fell into silence, considering the words of the wolf god. It was Idonea who broke the silence.

"Fenrir," Idonea said, glancing to Y'arren, who nodded. "I was actually going to seek you out, to request your help. I was wondering if you would deign to speak with me privately?"

"Of course, dragon's daughter," Fenrir said in his low rumble.

Fenrir loomed even larger in Idonea's chambers, and she admired his physique in wolf form. Drakar had watched them depart moodily, and perhaps with good cause as Idonea idly wondered what it would be like to have sex with a god. She then had the even more illicit thought of wondering what it would be like to have sex with him in his wolf form, then reflected on whether that was even physically possible. She then shook her head, trying to clear the image of Fenrir mounting her from behind. Her mother's dalliance with the gods had proved disastrous; she should take a lesson from that.

Fenrir seemed aware of, if not the totality of her thoughts, at least their general substance. He shifted uncomfortably and brushed his paw against his cheek, a gesture that was so endearing for a god, Idonea's thoughts went right back to where they had been a minute before. It was darling to see a creature of such power exhibit such a dour bashfulness. And Idonea had long wondered if the wolf god held some feeling for Raine beyond mere friendship.

Raine. The thought of her endangered friend immediately returned Idonea to focus.

"Fenrir, can you describe how you met Raine?"

Raine had described it to Idonea briefly, many years ago, and one aspect of the story had intrigued her.

"Of course," Fenrir said. "Not quite three centuries ago, I was trapped by three Sinisters."

"Sinisters?" Idonea said in surprise. Now she was intrigued by more than one aspect. "I thought that coven had died out eons ago."

"As did I," Fenrir said. The powerful witches had once terrorized Arianthem, using a combination of spells, enchantments, curses, and alchemy to petrify the common people. They pre-dated many of the races of Arianthem, and even the elves gave these sorceresses a wide berth, fearing the necromancy they practiced with ease.

"The Sinisters roamed this world with impunity for a thousand years," Fenrir said, "when the people were vulnerable to superstition and afraid of the dark."

"But it wasn't just superstition, the Sinisters possessed real power." Idonea said.

"Oh yes," Fenrir said, "they were deadly. It was only through the sustained efforts of one race that they were hunted down into extinction."

"What race was that?" Idonea asked, already guessing the answer.

"The Scinterians," Fenrir said. "Their resistance to magic was higher than any other people, and their physical strength grew from generation-to-generation. It is little-known, but their ceremony, the one in which Raine acquired her markings, grew from their conflict with the Sinisters."

"In what way?" Idonea asked, now fascinated with the story for a host of reasons beyond her original query.

"The ceremony was indeed designed to inflict such pain in a young Scinterian that they need fear nothing else in their life, having already borne the worst. But the blue and gold minerals they used, their identity and exact combination a closely-guarded secret, served a secondary purpose."

"And what purpose was that?"

"It prevented them from being raised from the dead."

Idonea considered his words. "So they were protected from the necromancy."

"They did not wish their undead form to battle their brethren."

That made sense, Idonea thought. Not only would it be horrible to have your corpse battle your loved ones, but an undead Scinterian would likely make a formidable foe.

"So a few of these Sinisters survived," Idonea mused.

"Yes, and I had warned them against using my children for their nefarious purposes. They did not take kindly to my threats, and trapped me."

Now this was the part of the story that had intrigued Idonea, even so many year ago.

"A magical trap?"

"Yes."

"But I thought that magic did not affect the gods."

"Extremely powerful magic can." Fenrir frowned. "And let's face it, despite my exalted relatives, I am not the most powerful of the pantheon."

"Can you describe the trap?"

"I remember it like it was yesterday. A pyramid-shaped cage made of red light, four sides coming to a point above my head."

"Were there any symbols written by the Sinisters?"

"Yes, written on the ground and in the light of the cage itself."

"Can you remember them, well enough to write down?"

"I spent months in that cage," Fenrir growled, "I believe that I can."

"Were there any smells that you can remember?"

"Sulfur," Fenrir answered, and Idonea nodded, "and something else. A type of burnt wood. I think it might have been juniper."

"Good," Idonea said, "that gives me a lot to start with."

Fenrir felt a vague unease about this line of questioning. "Can I ask you what you intend to do with this spell?"

Idonea was not certain whether or not to share her plan with the wolf god, but Raine trusted him absolutely.

"I intend to trap Hel with it."

"What?" Fenrir exclaimed. The audacity of the statement was staggering.

"I doubt that it will hold her for very long, but we will not need very long. Just enough time to escape with Raine and my mother."

"So you are going to march into the Underworld, trap the Goddess with magic, and free Raine and Talan?"

"Yes."

"You do realize there are hundreds of thousands of Hyr'rok'kin," Fenrir said, shaking his mane, "demons, demi-gods, specters, and other creatures in the Underworld, all that answer to Hel without question?"

"Yes, but that's not my problem. I was given a singular task, and that is the one I'm working on."

Fenrir considered the mage's words. Perhaps audacity was the only thing that would work in this situation. Traditional tactics would be useless.

"Well," he said, "regardless of the multitude of Hel's followers, you still have the most difficult task of all."

"I am aware of that," Idonea said.

Chapter 15

Raine rolled over in the sheets, her surroundings coming into focus. Although alone in the bed, she was not entirely alone, as Feray sat next to the volcanic rock frame, waiting for her to awaken.

"The Goddess is already in court," the handmaiden said, "and has commanded your presence upon your awakening."

Raine rubbed her eyes. Hel had been particularly insatiable last night, and Raine, once having fully satisfied her, passed into an unconscious sleep. Feray had sat contemplating Raine as she slept, the captive enjoying yet one more privilege she was oblivious to. The Goddess had arisen, enjoyed the sight of her exhausted lover tangled in the sheets, then went about her day, leaving the Arlanian to her handmaiden's charge.

Raine rose from the bed. She knew better than to argue with Feray. The woman wielded an enormous amount of power as only underlings can do. But Raine also knew how to unbalance her, and she did so now by pulling herself from the bed and padding across the floor barefoot and completely naked. Even Feray was affected by the Arlanian's charisma and watched the muscular form settle into the bath, desire twisting inside her torso. She forcefully suppressed the urge to go bathe the woman, knowing such an act might result in her destruction.

Raine cleaned herself quickly, methodically, taking little pleasure from the bath other than the warmth of the water, which felt good on her perennially cold skin. She scrubbed herself harshly, her thoughts elsewhere, and handmaidens appeared with black towels. She stepped from the pool, ignoring their stares, and dried herself in the same brusque manner. The clothing that Feray presented was beautiful, and Raine donned it without argument, those disputes having proved futile and a waste of time. She ran her fingers through her fair hair, and the handmaidens marveled that the simple gesture had as much effect as hours before a mirror: the hair was tousled, even a little unkempt, and wildly attractive.

Feray motioned for Raine to join her on the balcony and Raine did so. Immediately, Hel's chin tilted upward, aware of her presence, and the eyes of everyone in the room followed the attention of their Queen. Raine started down the steps, eyes forward, ignoring everyone around her as she stalked through the throng. Despite her disregard of everything in the room, she had made this trek so many times now that she recognized the "regulars." There was the woman with the greenish skin and enormous breasts, a creature half-sprite and half-serpent, the lower part slithering about on the floor, the upper part leaning across Raine's path as if to thrust those breasts in her face. Raine could not fathom the union that had produced this monstrosity. There were the various nobles in their finery, men and women who could pass in any court in the mortal realm, although there was always something slightly "off" about them, a sinister expression, a twisted gleam in their eye, a maniacal tinge to their polite laughter.

But the demons were the worst. Although most in the court had accepted Hel's elevation of the newcomer, the demons, through sheer stubbornness, still resisted. They were the least likely to hide their lust as the Arlanian walked through their midst, the most likely to whisper behind her back, and the most likely to attempt to threaten and intimidate Raine. This did not seem to bother Hel; it was simply the price of doing business with abhorrent creatures who had no morality, no scruples, and very little intelligence. Faen proved a remarkable exception, but most of the demons were only slightly more intelligent than the Hyr'rok'kin.

Raine saw one particularly large demon crowding the edge of her path. Orso'a was the foulest, and he took greater liberties because he was a consistent champion in the gladiatorial contests. He wore only a loin cloth and his enormous chest and shoulders were granite-like, a perception magnified by the grayish color of his skin. His biceps bulged and his forearms corded in a threatening manner as Raine neared. His brutish features leered down at her.

Raine's jaw tightened as she brushed past him, but she did not slow or deviate from her path. She fully expected him to make some revolting comment, but his words were despicable even for him.

"Fucked a lot of Arlanians," Orso'a sneered, "maybe even your mother."

Raine stopped, and the great hall grew very quiet. Hel could not hear the exchange, but she sat upright at the abrupt halt and sudden tension in the mortal's body.

Raine turned around, looking up at the gigantic demon.

"What did you just say?"

Those nearest the demon and the mortal shifted uneasily and many took a step back. Orso'a was deadly, and although sworn to Hel's service, could be unpredictable. A few glanced to Hel, who seemed on the verge of putting a stop to the scene. But Orso'a had hated the mortal on sight, a hatred fueled by jealousy, lust, and a sense of inferiority only amplified by Hel's obvious favor of the weakling. He had been waiting for this opportunity and would press forward before it was stolen from him.

"I said, I fucked a lot of Arlanians, maybe even your mother. I might even have some little half-demon, bitch-Arlanians running around here."

Raine reached up and slapped the demon, a move so startlingly fast that Orso'a could not quite comprehend the sting on his flesh.

"I challenge you for insulting my honor."

Orso'a smiled, revealing a row of sharpened fangs. He rubbed the sting on his cheek. "You have no standing here. You have no honor to defend."

Hel stood up to stop the situation from unraveling further when Raine said the only thing that would stay her hand.

"Then I will fight for her honor."

All eyes turned to the Goddess of the Underworld, for that was where Raine was pointing. Slowly, Hel sat back down. Although her expression was impassive, Hel was furious and her emerald eyes glowed with that wrath. That idiot demon had orchestrated this situation and the Arlanian had neatly trapped her. Although few were allowed to declare themselves her champion, the fact that the girl sat at her side gave the declaration instant legitimacy. And to stop the challenge now would bring grave insult. Hel wanted to strike down Orso'a due to his stupidity and insolence, and she wanted to punish the Arlanian for her insubordination. But, as she settled on the throne and smoothed her robes about her, she had to admit one thing: she stayed her hand as much from uncertainty as from a preservation of honor. She was curious as to how exactly this would play out, and was the only one in the room who thought the mortal stood even a chance.

Orso'a sensed none of his Queen's fury, or her doubt, and he sought only to push the Arlanian further. "You don't seem to have any weapons."

And this angered Raine more than anything, even more so than the childish taunts regarding her mother. Orso'a wore her weapons at his side. Raine had no idea how he had obtained them, but he brandished them as trophies he hadn't earned, for he had not been at the battle in Nifelheim. Each time she had entered the court, she had passed him and felt her anger burn at his possession of her most cherished items. She had shifted restlessly as he had fought for the entertainment of all with the dual swords tempered in a Scinterian forge. And the object swinging from his belt, the one that he clearly had no idea how to use, was the one she desired most of all.

"I'm going to kill you with that," Raine said, pointing at the metallic object.

"This?" Orso'a said, reaching down.

But he was not fast enough, for in a move that was indescribable in speed, Raine snatched the object from his waist, flicked her wrist in a violent movement, snapped the risers out to their full-lengths, and spun the weapon into position. The strange-looking object was a Scinterian bow, deadly as a ranged weapon but just as deadly in melee combat. As Orso'a was drawing the double swords, Raine stepped sideways and swept the wickedly-sharp leading edge downward across the back of his leg, severing all the tendons at the knee. The swords came out but the giant was already hobbled, and Raine swept his other knee. He stumbled, swinging the swords, but Raine drew a beautiful arc in the air, trapping the sword nearest her, then slicing down with the bow and cutting the tendons at the elbow. It was a Scinterian battle tactic to cripple a much larger opponent if possible, and Orso'a was not wearing armor. Raine's precision was such that the demon's overpowering strength was removed as a factor.

Still, her rage drove her to unleash her own unnatural strength, and with a flip of the wrist, the bow was retracted, tucked into her sash, and she moved to snatch the sword dangling from the demon's injured arm. She twisted the appendage and Orso'a screamed. She stepped forward into his looming bulk, closing the distance between them, and blocked the clumsy attack from the demon's other hand. Forearm to forearm, she then sliced the tendons of that elbow as well with her still-free sword hand. The demon screamed again in fury and pain, but he did not scream for long as Raine snatched the other sword, then flipped them about her wrists in a dazzling flurry. She crossed the blades, one on each side of his thick neck, and pulled them apart with such violence it severed his head cleanly and sent it halfway across the room.

The great hall went completely silent. Hel sat on her throne, elbow on her arm rest, her index finger pressed against her cheek and her chin propped upon her hand, a look of mild exasperation on her face, but little if any surprise at the outcome.

Those surrounding the Arlanian, who had just been forcefully reminded that she was also Scinterian, moved back, for the mortal was still armed and seething with anger. Raine sought to control herself, for it was certain the Goddess would not allow her any more leeway. Hel glanced to Faen, and he grimaced at her implicit command. He started down the steps, having received the unenviable task of disarming the deadly creature. He stopped a short distance from Raine, and the court guards all raised their pikes so that they hovered in her direction, although their positioning appeared more defensive than threatening. Faen's tail wavered taut just above the ground, the appendage ready to flee even if its master did not. Finally, Raine turned towards the demon, flicked the swords about her wrists in a snapping movement that made Faen flinch, and handed them to him hilt first. She removed the bow from her sash and shoved it towards his chest. He juggled the weapons before securing them.

"Make sure my weapons are cleaned," she said, then turned and dismissed him, walking away. For once, Faen took the dismissal with more relief than anger.

Raine made her way up the steps, her eyes lowered. Hel watched the approach, entertained. Feray stepped forward and Raine took the cloth she extended. She wiped a small spot of blood from her cheek, then returned the cloth to the handmaiden. Raine then took her place at Hel's side, sitting down without speaking a word.

Hel enjoyed the sulky, brooding look of her captive for a moment, particularly the pouty fullness it gave her lips. This could not have worked out more perfectly for her ultimate plans for the mortal. She returned her attention to the court, her thoughts pleasantly elsewhere. If the Arlanian thought last night had been challenging, she should prepare herself for a night to remember.

Raine collapsed upon the Goddess, breathing much harder than she had in her battle with Orso'a. She was bathed in sweat, her Scinterian markings livid upon her skin. Hel had given her a phallus, some infernal, cursed device which intensified her pleasure even more than usual, and seemed to drive Hel to heights of unmatched ecstasy. Now her heart beat like a hummingbird against her chest wall.

Hel brushed the damp hair at the nape of Raine's neck, then began tracing the blue and gold markings on that muscular back. Her pleasure had little to do with Sjöfn's toy. The Arlanian had been nearly violent in her love-making, driven by anger, desire, and passion, none of which she could control. Hel had sensed her attempt to engage her Scinterian side, and for once, simply let her do it. The outcome was not what Raine had hoped and exactly what Hel had expected. She continued to trace the markings, almost mockingly.

"Do you really think I don't know what you were trying to do?" Hel murmured into her ear.

Raine remained mute, her heart finally beginning to slow its frantic beating against the breasts of the Goddess.

"You thought if you could bring forth the Scinterian in you, you might gain some semblance of control."

A muscle jumped in Raine's cheek as she stared at the black sheets, still silent.

"The truth of the matter," Hel continued, "is that I will enjoy that half of you as much as the other."

Hel rolled Raine over onto her back and stared down into violet eyes, then down at the blue and gold markings that curved over the top of the shoulders. She leaned down to kiss the beautiful scars. She then kissed her lips, luxuriating in the purple depths as she spoke her decree.

"And now both belong to me."

When Raine awoke, it was to find her weapons hanging on the wall of the adjacent room, encased in some type of hardened sap, much like relics from the past could be trapped in amber. She could see them from the bed, hung on the slanted walls. It seemed the shrine would now serve as a trophy room as well.

The thought of a trophy room disturbed Raine in some instinctual way, and the disquiet roused her from the bed. She pulled on the clothing that had been left her, and found her steps drawn to the Tree of Death in the garden. The sap of the monstrosity glowed ominously in the dim light in front of her. She sat down on the bench in front of the tree and pondered the unease that those heavy curtains caused her. Every attempt to move the massive coverings had failed. She could no more budge them than the heavy door that was the only viable exit from Hel's chambers.

Raine's thoughts, and then her gaze, drifted to the darkness surrounding her, the vast emptiness that bordered the garden. It had become tempting of late. At first she had tried to push these thoughts from her mind, dismissing them as cowardly and suicidal. But lately, she more considered escape into that oblivion. She tried to rationalize the pull of the darkness, telling herself that perhaps she could survive where others had not. But the rationalizations were unconvincing, the traitorous lures of despair, and she would not risk ending it all when she did not know the fate of her love. Somewhere, Weynild was still alive, and that was the only thing she could hold onto when the importance of all else had faded.

Feray approached her quietly from behind. Raine made the slightest movement of her head, acknowledging her presence.

"I have a message from the Goddess."

Raine stared at the golden sap that ran down the trunk of the tree like blood from an open wound.

"Yes?"

"She was greatly pleased by your victory over Orso'a, and the honor it brought her name."

Raine's jaw clenched as she stared mutely at the rivulets of gold. It was just as likely the Goddess was pleased by the fact she had fucked her into mindless ecstasy.

"She has offered you a gift," Feray continued, "anything you might desire."

"So she will free me?" Raine asked sarcastically.

"You know the answer to that," Feray said.

Raine did indeed know the answer to that. Hel offered her anything she desired that did not interfere with her own desires. Raine immediately shut out any idea of asking about Weynild. Those questions were perilous in every way, including a threat to her own sanity. She would ask nothing from the Goddess about her beloved.

She considered asking for her weapons back, but that, too, was futile. It was unlikely the weapons would be of any use against a god, but Raine had proven herself more than capable of taking down the other denizens of the Underworld. She might not escape, but she could wreak a glorious havoc, which Hel would not allow.

Raine could think of nothing she wanted that the Goddess would be willing to give her. Where so many others had wished for wealth, or special abilities, or fame, she wanted none of these things. She looked up at the foreign stars that had grown no more familiar to her during her lengthy stay.

"I know what I want."

Feray turned to her in surprise. She fully expected to return to the Goddess with no response, at least none that would be acceptable to her Majesty.

"These stars," Raine said, "the ones here and in the chambers, I want them to be the ones over Arianthem."

Feray considered the request. It was minimal, requiring no effort at all on the part of the Goddess, and it did not seem likely to raise her ire. If anything, she might be irritated that the Arlanian had asked for so little. She nodded, then left Raine alone in the garden.

Raine reclined on the bench to look up at the night sky. She could not see Feray as she made her way down the steps into the court, nor when she made her way back up the staircase to the dais. She could not see the handmaiden pause at the side of the throne to whisper in the ear of the

Goddess. She could not see Hel consider the request, sigh and roll her eyes, then wave her hand imperiously. But she did see the immediate result of that command.

The stars above her shifted dramatically, as if she had traveled an enormous distance between worlds. And then they settled into familiar patterns and constellations, giving Raine her location, the time of year, a sense of direction, and so many other comforting orientations that, false or not, she felt a sense of peace settle over her that she had not felt since she left the mortal realm. She lay on her back staring up at the stars for hours, and the handmaidens all commented on her dreamy smile, and the violet of her eyes that was almost as dark as the night sky.

Chapter 16

The focus of the Tavinter was total, and Idonea was impressed. Skye had entered her magical training relatively late in her young life, and less than enthusiastically, thinking herself untalented. Even upon learning that she was from Isleif's line, she still preferred her bow and sword. But Raine's capture and Talan's disappearance had instilled in her a resolve and determination that was astonishing. Skye's power, and more importantly, her control of that power, was growing every day. Right now, she had made a large portion of the garden invisible, and an even larger part of it ephemeral, all the while balancing an orb of light on her palm that frosted the air around it with its frigid temperature.

"Good," Idonea said. "Your ability to sustain multiple spells is improving."

It was a complete understatement. Skye was sustaining multiple spells that no one else could even cast. But when your great-grandfather was the greatest wizard Arianthem had ever known, your instructor was the most powerful mage in Arianthem, your lover an indomitable sorceress, and your mentor a revered elven seer who was master of the natural world, extraordinary accomplishment felt expected and routine. Skye's modesty added to the lack of fanfare, and Idonea was thankful for that humility, for she had seen far less skilled mages corrupted by far less power.

Skye released all of the spells and the garden reappeared. She was careful to ensure that no one would be affected by the return of the ephemeral objects. Someone could walk into an invisible object, for it was still present, but would walk right through one that was ephemeral. This could be dangerous if the object materialized while they were occupying the same space. She meant to speak with Idonea about the possibility of using this quirk as a weapon.

"You should rest for a bit," Idonea said. She nodded to Lifa, who was strolling into the garden with Ama and Freya, priestesses on her staff, in tow. Lifa waved to Skye and approached Y'arren, who sat on a bench near the opening of her tent. Skye watched curiously as Lifa spoke with the ancient elf, and saw Y'arren smile. The matriarch gestured to her attendant, who disappeared through the flap of the tent, then returned bearing a scroll and a quill. Y'arren wrote something very carefully on the scroll, blessed it, waited for it to dry, then handed it to Lifa with great gravity. Lifa hugged the scroll to her chest, thanked Y'arren, and started toward Skye.

Skye wiped the sweat from her brow and returned the embroidered handkerchief to her pocket.

"Hello, my love," Lifa said, beaming. She kissed Skye firmly on the mouth, a kiss Skye fully returned. The Tavinter then kneeled almost reverently before her and kissed the unborn child. She caressed the swollen belly for a moment, then rose to her feet once more.

"What was that about?" Skye asked, nodding towards the scroll.

"This contains the name of my daughter."

This brought smiles all around, even to the somber Skye. "Your daughter? But how does Y'arren know the name of your daughter?"

"I wanted to honor Raine," Lifa said, "so I asked her the name of Raine's mother."

This brought a touch of sadness to Skye's smile, but only a touch because it was a wonderful idea.

"And so what will be the name of your daughter?" she asked.

"It is fabulous," Lifa said, unrolling the scroll and gazing at the name that could not have been more perfect.

"Her name will be Serene."

•

Chapter 17

K iren chewed her lip, something she did when she was deep in thought, and also when she was on the verge of discovery. Both of those situations were in play at the moment. She had been working feverishly on translating the final line of the prophecy and felt very close to the solution. The Lady Jorden, one of the few humans Maeva called friend, had recently provided a key manunscript, one "borrowed" by her very talented lover Syn, a master thief. This relic was proving a bridge between eras.

There was no direct line from this ancient language to present languages, so she had to trace meanings and nuances from one tongue, find their equivalent in another, then trace that to a third. She continued this leap from language to language through centuries, always mindful that her interpretation was as accurate as possible. Much like the mathematics of archery, a small deviation at the source would result in wild inaccuracy over a great distance.

The lip suffered from her absorption once more, and she pulled a dusty tome from the stack that teetered precariously to her right. She eyed it as it threatened to topple, then swayed back into an unsteady compromise with gravity. She turned her attention back to the tome set before her. She opened the fragile pages carefully, then began tracing her finger down the graceful symbols and marks.

The finger slowed, then stopped. A frown curved the corners of her mouth and her brow furrowed. Kiren stared down at the symbols in front of her, reading, then re-reading the phrase before her. She pulled another tome from her left, opened it to a bookmarked page, and compared the two. She repeated this process with a third, and then a fourth, cross-referencing her discovery. She then returned to the dusty tome, staring down, her eyes filled with an enigmatic and uncharacteristic darkness.

The teetering stack of books lost its battle with gravity and fell over with a crash, causing Kiren to jump. An elven guard leaned into the room to check on her.

"Is everything alright?"

Kiren gathered herself. She pulled a sheet of parchment to her and dipped a quill in ink.

"Yes," she said, writing in a flurry. "I need to send a message to Y'arren."

Chapter 18

Raine sat at the side of the Goddess, looking out over the assembly with a vacant stare. Any boost she had received from killing Orso'a had dissipated. Fenrir's visit had left her morose, lethargic, and those feelings returned once the thrill of her battle with the demon had waned. Every hour she did not spend with Hel, she spent walking in the garden, trying to generate energy and trying to ignore the beckoning darkness that surrounded her. She exercised, moved boulders about, pulled herself up into the trees, performed sword drills with branches, and generally provided much entertainment for Hel's handmaidens, who loved to watch her move. These periods of activity ended when the Goddess arrived, for she, too, liked to watch Raine move, and her desire would rise, the handmaidens would be dismissed, and any energy Raine expended would be in bed.

But now Raine sat lethargic once more, her disinterest in the proceedings pronounced. Hel did not care. It was only necessary for the Arlanian to sit at her side obediently. She did, however, feel a small trace of victory when she caught the slight tilt of Raine's chin that betrayed interest in something occurring. The gladiatorial contests were beginning, and it seemed the one thing to which her captive was attentive. Of course, Orso'a was no longer competing, which did not make them any less entertaining, but did cause many in the audience to glance up at the mortal, remembering her effortless defeat of the previous champion.

The contests were brutal, the combatants fighting for revenge, retaliation, honor, and Raine would have competed in them for no reason at all, given the chance. But it was clear her one foray into combat was over. Hel would not allow Raine to leave her side, and certainly would not allow any weapons back into her hands.

So Raine watched the combatants, mentally critiquing their style, analyzing their technique, cataloguing everything should she ever wind up fighting a similar opponent. She inwardly crafted defenses, counter attacks, strategies for defeating them one at a time, or even for fighting them all at once. It was far more entertaining for her than anything else she experienced in the Underworld, and it was one of the few things that could engross her enough so she forgot where she was.

As Raine watched the competition, Feray watched her. The evolution of the relationship between this mortal and the Goddess was fascinating. Feray began to notice a difference in Hel. The Goddess was no less arrogant or imperious in her treatment of her underlings, but she was less mercurial. In judgment, Hel was no more merciful, but she was more just. And it was not merely Feray who noticed the changes in Hel. Many in the court noted the subtle alterations in the behavior of the Goddess, and silently began to welcome the presence of the Arlanian, despite its involuntary nature.

The competition ended, and Raine escorted the Goddess from the throne room as required. Raine sought to escape into the garden, but she was stopped by Hel's voice.

"I have not dismissed you."

Although Raine stopped, Feray noted her stubborn posture and faded into the background, motioning for the handmaidens to do the same. This was a pattern she recognized well. The Arlanian would begin to chafe beneath her invisible bonds, Hel's irritation would grow, the mortal would rebel, and it would end explosively, usually in violence or bed, or most of the time, in both.

"Might I go into the garden?" Raine said, clenching her teeth.

"No," Hel said, "you may not."

The indignity of being refused was even greater than that of having to ask. Raine struggled with herself, then lost the battle. She took a step toward the garden.

"I said no," Hel said, her emerald eyes furious. She raised her hand, stopping Raine instantly. Raine fought against the sensation, but could not move. She still did not understand the power of the gods, and every muscle in her body strained against some invisible force. Her forearms corded, the muscles in her thighs bunched, and she struggled to move to no avail.

The fact that she even tried angered Hel further. With a wave of her hand, she snatched Raine forward like a rag doll, dragging her across the room until she stood before her. With another toss of her hand, Raine was on her back in the bed, and a wave of Hel's wrist ripped the clothing from her body. Hel stalked over to her, staring down at that magnificent form, trying to control her wrath. She knew that the mortal pushed her on purpose, preferred that she would hurt her instead of bring her pleasure, and for exactly those reasons Hel would not. But she could do other things.

The Membrane floated in from the garden, and the handmaidens, who all hovered in the alcoves, could not look away. It would be glorious to watch the monstrosity pleasure the Arlanian, for the Membrane would not harm one it so evidently craved. Raine felt her body temperature drop precipitously, still unable to move under Hel's restraint. The amalgam of limbs and breasts and lips hovered over her, fairly shivering in delight. The creature fluttered, nipples hardened about its surface, a phallus grew erect, a pair of lips lowered to settle between her legs, and Raine turned her head away, closing her eyes in misery.

Hel banished the creature. She stood gazing down at her captive until those eyes reopened, then removed her robes so that the eyes would turn violet for her. Hel lowered herself gently onto Raine, who still could barely move and whose skin was so deliciously cold. The violet eyes stared up in despair.

"You have no idea the plans I have for you," Hel said, still angry, "the glories I will offer you."

"I want nothing from you," Raine said.

"What you want," Hel said, biting off the words, "does not matter."

A black, smoky tendril appeared behind Hel and snaked its way over her shoulder. Raine tried to pull away but still could not. She eyed it as it trailed down Hel's torso, then settled on her own. It was soft, possessing a presence and substance that real smoke did not. It caressed Raine, tracing her rib cage to her breast, then feathering the nipple which hardened in response. A second tendril curled down over Hel's other shoulder, also stroking Raine's skin, then settling on the other breast and provoking the same physical reaction. Raine tried to push Hel away as more tendrils appeared, snaking around her body from every direction, and Hel merely laughed and leaned down to kiss her. The Goddess probed her mouth with her tongue as the dark wisps probed Raine's body, gliding over her skin in delighted exploration. It was as if the blackness in Hel had manifested in perverse form and now sought to please them both, for the dark tendrils were masturbatory in their exploration of the Goddess. She sighed in pleasure as one penetrated her and began a gentle thrusting that caused her to bury her tongue in the Arlanian's mouth and grind against the hard body beneath her.

Feray watched from the alcove, having had every intention of leaving, but now unable to look away. The mortal fought to resist the onslaught, but it was clear by the arms that came up around the Goddess, freed from Hel's paralysis, that the mortal lost the battle as she had every time before. Hel laughed in delight as the strong legs wrapped around her, the kiss was passionately returned, and the hips moved in response to the stroking of the black smoke that so perfectly coordinated their rhythms into one. Feray felt her own control crumble as everything between her legs became alive and tingled, a wetness flowed into her undergarments, and her nipples strained against her robes. For once, the servility of Hel's creations was a blessing, for when the carnal creature crouching next to Feray in the alcove tugged at the hem of her robe, a questioning look in her eyes, Feray did not hesitate. She swept the robes to the side and grabbed the woman's head, and the hungry mouth latched onto the wetness between her legs in an explosion of sensation. Feray rode the lips and tongue, her back against the stone wall of the alcove, clutching the head as if to never let it go. Her only regret, as she erupted into the handmaiden's mouth, was that she could no longer see Hel or the Arlanian, for they were engulfed in a writhing swarm of complete and total darkness.

Chapter 19

The cage of light glowed a sinister red, the bars sparking with energy, the structure humming with power. Y'arren watched Idonea carefully, making sure that the mage did not lose control or that the strain was not too much for her. The dragon's daughter was under great duress, that much was apparent, but she appeared capable of maintaining the spell.

Skye sat on a bench nearby, fingering the filigreed edge of its marble surface. She brushed her hair from her eyes, her expression pensive as she watched Idonea.

"That will not hold Hel."

Skye turned in surprise to the woman sitting next to her, the sorceress who had appeared out of thin air. Ingrid often used enchanted artifacts to open portals to cut through Nifelheim, for her soul was dark enough to attract little attention from the evil that thrived there, and she was not enough of a threat to warrant any of Hel's attention. And the sorceress was keeping a much more fluid schedule than they had agreed upon, showing up really whenever the mood struck her. She only demanded blood upon the full moon, but sex was something she required more often, a condition that did not bother Skye in the least.

Skye's surprise, therefore, was not that Ingrid had appeared, but that she had instantly deduced both the spell and its purpose, something that was closely guarded from all save the handful of people present. The Tavinter was uncertain how to feel about this breach in security, mirroring the uncertainty she felt about the sorceress in general.

The dark presence of the sorceress imprinted upon Y'arren instantly, and she, too, gazed at the woman with reservation. No one knew the extent of Ingrid's role in Raine's capture, but Y'arren sensed it was significant. Only Y'arren's deep intuition kept her from banishing the woman from the garden. The elven seer sensed regret intertwined with the secret the sorceress held so tight, and the search for redemption could be a powerful motivating force.

Ingrid examined the symbols drawn in the air, recognizing many of the ancient glyphs from her own research. It was a marvelous contraption, she had to admit, drawn from some malevolent imagination to be sure.

Idonea was also aware of Ingrid's arrival, but her focus was entirely on the magical trap. The slightest waver in her concentration could be treacherous, for the spell was so dark there was no telling what would happen if she lost control of it. It had to be ended in a methodical and orderly manner, which she did so now, deconstructing the trap glyph-by-glyph until the cage itself winked out of existence, leaving only a crackling in the air behind. She relaxed once the crackling ceased.

Her admiration for the spell and the dragon's daughter irritated Ingrid. The raven-haired mage had battled her as none other, drawing from the deep well of dark magic that ran through her blood. The fact that the mage was so much younger than Ingrid and had trained with Isleif as his protégé made the involuntary admiration all the more unpalatable. Although Ingrid cared little about Skye's sexual partners, when the girl revealed, upon Ingrid's interrogation, that she had not slept with the mage, Ingrid was greatly relieved. Although, the sorceress mused, examining the breasts that spilled forth from Idonea's plunging bodice, she would probably fuck her if given the chance.

"That will not hold Hel," Ingrid repeated, louder this time.

"I am aware of that," Idonea said, too fatigued to respond with her usual sarcasm. "It will not even hold Fenrir at the moment."

This was of interest to Ingrid, and gave her possible insight as to where Idonea had obtained the spell. She had long-wondered at the relationship between the Scinterian and the wolf god. Rumor held that the warrior had saved him from a magical trap. Ingrid now wondered if Idonea was seeking to replicate that trap.

Skye felt a profound unease at the silent musings of the woman next to her, and cast a troubled glance Y'arren's way. Ingrid had sided with the Goddess once. Skye's arrangement with the sorceress had satisfied her lust for pleasure, but her lust for power was unabated. Another deal with the Goddess might satisfy that hunger.

"Oh, don't look at me that way," Ingrid said, glancing down at her young companion. The Tavinter could hide nothing; everything they thought and felt was written on their face. "Cast it again," Ingrid said, turning back to Idonea. Her professional curiosity was getting the best of her.

Idonea sent a questioning look Y'arren's way, and the old elf simply nodded. Idonea composed herself, then began constructing the cage, symbol by symbol, once more. That was one problem that had to be overcome. Right now, the casting of the spell was piece-by-piece, taking a length of time that was totally impractical. Hel was not going to stand around while Idonea finished the job. Eventually, she was going to have to cast it instantaneously, in one smooth motion.

But today, Idonea still built the glowing cage of light one wall at a time, finally sealing the pyramid at the top. It crackled and popped, the energy seething against its invisible constraints. Idonea took a deep breath and stabilized the spell.

Ingrid examined the glyphs, mentally translating their various raw meanings and seeing the pattern they formed to build the trap. It really was quite ingenious and she determined she would prod the mage until she gave up their origins. But right now she was more interested in their combination, the configuration that produced the end result. One glyph leaped out at her, not for its power or originality, but because it did not seem quite right.

"This one," Ingrid said, moving closer to Idonea and pointing at one symbol, "something is wrong with this one."

"I am open to suggestions," Idonea said, her sarcasm returning despite the strain of maintaining the spell.

Ingrid stared at the glyph. It was familiar, and yet not. Something was slightly off, and her thoughts began to wander. If, as she suspected, Fenrir had given Idonea these glyphs, he must have done so from memory. And if he had seen them when he was trapped, then he had seen them only from the inside of the cage...

"Flip it," Ingrid said, "from left to right. I think it is backwards."

Y'arren leaned forward. If the sorceress was incorrect, it could have devastating consequences. If it was an act of sabotage, it was one that they might not recover from if Idonea was injured or unthinkably, killed. Nothing told Y'arren to stay Idonea's hand, but her misgivings for her inaction were great. Skye, too, stood up from the bench, prepared to do something, but with no idea of what. Both waited to see what Idonea would do, leaving the decision to her.

The glowing glyph floated before Idonea as she considered her next move and its repercussions. All of the possible motivations of the sorceress were in play. Most of the potential outcomes of the action were bad. The endless branching of possibilities was making her head hurt. Finally, despite her newfound maturity, patience, and discipline, she reverted to her natural state of reckless action.

"Well, fuck it," she muttered, and waved her hand.

The glyph flipped and all present held their breath. But the result was almost anticlimactic. The crackling stopped and settled into a low thrumming as the spell stabilized. The red light, already brilliant, brightened further and seemed to throb like a heartbeat. The cage itself seemed to harden, taking on a near-solid form.

"You can thank me later," Ingrid said, and the glance at Idonea's cleavage communicated how she wished to be paid. Idonea was again reminded of her mother's caution that magical energy and sexual energy were likely two sides of the same coin, marveling at how wise that old dragon was.

Ingrid turned about, reveling in her triumph, a rarity in this present company.

"That was entertaining," she said as she took Skye's hand, "but I'm in the mood for a different kind of entertainment."

Skye grasped the hand and dutifully followed her from the garden while Y'arren was left to ponder the Tavinter's relationship with her dark paramour, contemplating all the twists and turns of fate.

Chapter 20

Raine sat in the garden, staring at the ground before her. The altercation with Hel and its aftermath had left her shaken and drained. Even now she shivered as she sat before the ominous tree. A handmaiden brought her a blanket and draped it over her shoulders, but she did not move or even acknowledge the gesture as she stared at the fluorescent plants before her without seeing them. The handmaiden faded away into the shadows. The quiet chirp of the birds did not register on Raine, and the gentle hum of the glowing insects faded away into her dark thoughts.

She felt broken, shattered into a million pieces. Her attempt to engage her Scinterian side had failed, only playing into Hel's hands further. She had no idea where Weynild was, if her friends had survived, or how the war had played out. For all she knew, Arianthem was utterly destroyed, or still under siege by that army of Hyr'rok'kin. She refused to ask about any of these things. She had long hoped she would hear some rumor in the court, or some whisper from the handmaidens, but no one spoke of such things, at least within her hearing.

Her physical attraction to Hel seemed to grow with every contact. She had been unable to resist the Goddess from the start, but now their couplings grew more and more intense. It did not matter what the Goddess did to her, she responded to her with a passion that was as degrading as it was uncontrolled. Raine was fearful she was beginning to lose herself in that passion, the continual waves of pleasure, the feelings that never touched her heart, but could erase everything else around her like a drug that provided euphoric rapture, then left one numb.

Her eyes flicked upward. The blackness at the edge of the garden beckoned invitingly, and Raine looked back down lest her interest in that wall of darkness could be seen. Both Feray and Faen had been watching her closely all morning, probably on some intuition of the Goddess. Indecision was mirrored on her face, but no one could see as her back was to all save the tree. She did not know what was in the emptiness, monsters, madness, or perhaps nothing at all, but she could no longer remain and do nothing. The hope that Weynild's fate would be revealed to her was dying. Her only solace was that her love could find her anywhere, even in that black oblivion.

She stood, pretending to examine the nearby plants in greater detail. She followed the line of plants, which brought her conveniently close to that forbidden boundary. She kneeled down, examining some glowing petals and fingering their silky texture, coming away with an iridescent powder on her fingertips. She rubbed the pollen between the pads of her index finger and thumb, then stood upright. She took a deep breath. It would take only three steps, and she would be swallowed by that great night.

She did not make it one.

"What are you doing?"

Hel stared down at her, having materialized directly in her path. Her emerald eyes were furious, and Raine knew that any excuse, really any words at all, would only make matters worse. Her arms were snatched by the demon guards that now stood on both sides of her, and they dragged her roughly away from the border of the garden.

"Unfortunate," Hel said, raising her arm, "for I have always enjoyed this view."

At the command of Hel's raised arm, a massive ebony wall rose up at the edge of the garden, churning the earth beneath it, enclosing the space entirely. It reached towards the night sky, blocking out all of the emptiness beyond. The garden now had a far more claustrophobic feel to it, having transitioned from an open air space to an enclosed courtyard. The one place that had felt like outdoors to Raine now felt like a prison.

Hel stalked by her, her black robes flowing behind her. "Bring her," she said icily.

Raine was half-dragged, half-carried by the demons who were feeding off the anger of their Mistress. Feray watched the escort of the prisoner with near pity. She had seen Hel in every phase of anger: irritation, annoyance, frustration, even rage, but she could not remember ever seeing such volcanic wrath on the face of the Goddess of the Underworld before. The demons dragged Raine up the stairs as she stumbled to get her footing, then shoved her into the room.

"In here," Hel said, moving into the shrine.

The demons complied, nearly pulling Raine's arms from her sockets as they dragged her across the floor, then threw her on the stone tiles in front of those great heavy curtains.

"Leave us," Hel commanded, and the demons disappeared.

Raine rubbed her arm where the guard had nearly dislocated her shoulder. She was still on her knees, uncertain if Hel would strike her if she got to her feet. But when she looked up, Hel's volcanic anger had transitioned to something different. Her fury was still present, but now it was tinged with self-satisfaction and a trace of triumph. The expression filled Raine with dread. She slowly got to her feet, still rubbing her shoulder.

"So willing to leave me after all we've shared?" Hel said sarcastically.

Raine said nothing as Hel stalked in a circle around her.

"Willing to walk into the blackness of oblivion?" Hel continued. "Willing to chance annihilation rather than share my bed?"

Raine maintained her silence, but the dread she was experiencing was only increasing. Hel was leading up to something, and whatever it was, it wasn't good.

"Then perhaps you should see what else you were willing to walk away from."

And with a great flourish, Hel swept one of the curtains aside, the massively heavy drape that Raine had been unable to budge. The curtain moved as if it weighed nothing, then fluttered to the floor. Raine stared in horror and disbelief at what lie beyond.

It was Weynild.

The dragon was in her human form, trapped in what looked like a block of amber only slightly lighter in color than her own golden eyes. Those eyes stared out expressionlessly, vacantly, the body immobilized in the hardened, petrified sap that looked exactly like that which oozed from the Tree of Death.

"That," Hel said triumphantly, "is what you would have left in my hands."

Y'arren received the courier carrying the missive from the Alfar Republic with great gravity. The young man was exhausted, having spared no time for rest in his long journey. The elven matriarch waved to her attendants to assist him, and turned her attention to the bundle he produced. Although the courier knew nothing of the content of the message, the mood and words of the Directorate's young companion had impressed themselves upon him, and this urgent solemnity was conveyed to Y'arren in an instant. She removed the scroll and carried it into her tent.

The graceful scrawl was familiar to Y'arren. The message was from Maeva's young prize, Kiren, the human lover who was a talented scholar and an expert in linguistics. But although the handwriting was familiar to Y'arren, the broad loops and the bold slashes of the writing was not, and they indicated that it had been written in great haste and agitation.

Y'arren's heart beat faster and she took a deep breath to calm herself. She read down through the missive carefully and methodically, resisting the urge to just skim through it. She absorbed Kiren's process, her step-by-step reasoning, her interim findings, and finally, she turned to the last page where the conclusions were written.

Her heart stopped. She read, then re-read the translation of the final line of the prophecy. She went back to the beginning of the letter, read through the entire thing again, especially Kiren's humble entreaties that her work be reviewed and vetted in the hope that she had made an error.

Y'arren slowly lowered the parchment. She knew that the brilliant little scholar had made no mistake. She would have her own sages review the work, of course, and she would do so personally, as well. But she knew that Kiren had translated the line properly.

"Is there something wrong?"

The elven attendant stood in the doorway, unwilling to disturb the matriarch, but moved by the stricken look on her face.

"We need to call the allies to a meeting," Y'arren said.

Raine stood before her entombed lover in stunned silence. She took a step forward, unable to process the sight of her beloved so close to her, yet still so impossibly far away. Weynild was in her armor and had her hand upright, as if to ward off whatever disaster had placed her in this state of suspension, caught in the pose right before her imprisonment. Raine slowly lifted her hand and pressed it against the transparent prison, inches from the hand of her love.

"The most prized trophy in my trophy room," Hel said, her rancor having dissolved into an amused sarcasm that was so much worse.

"What have you done to her?"

"She is not dead," Hel said, moving to examine her prize. "She is encased in the hardened resin from the tree you sit before in my garden." Hel's tone was perversely casual. "I feared it might kill her, but dragons can hibernate for centuries, even millennia, and so she lies dormant as a protection against the draining of the substance." She gazed at the beautiful regal features that stared out at nothing. "It was exactly what I expected to happen."

Hel's self-satisfied exposition tore at Raine like a jagged blade. She pressed her forehead against the amber in anguish. Hel's pleasure at her agony was almost as great as the pleasure of viewing Talan so powerless.

"You once asked me," she continued, stepping away from the encased dragon, "why I didn't kill you."

Raine tensed at this change in conversation, thinking Hel was going to speak of the bond between her and Weynild, fearing that somehow she had discovered their connection.

"You said you did not want to turn me into a thrall."

"Well, that was certainly part of the reason," Hel said, "but I did not tell you the truth in its entirety."

Raine turned to the Goddess, who was now toying with the cord of the other curtain. "I needed to keep you alive so that you could fulfill your prophecy."

"My prophecy?" Raine said bitterly. "My prophecy has hardly been fulfilled."

"Oh," Hel said, her sense of triumph filling Raine with even more dread, which hardly seemed possible, "I'm afraid that it has."

Hel swept aside the second curtain with the same ease, and the cloth that Raine could not budge again fluttered to the ground. There was no horrific revelation this time, no loved one encased in amber like some insect, merely a stone wall with primeval markings on it that resembled ancient elvish. But Raine's sense of dread had not diminished a whit, but continued to grow with an almost suffocating intensity.

Hel waved her hand, and the first line of ancient symbols lit up in glowing outlines, then resolved themselves into the common tongue. Although Raine could easily read it now, Hel took great pleasure in reading it for her.

"The Dragon's Lover," she began, with a significant glance at Raine, then at Weynild. She waved her hand, and the second line on the wall jumped to life, then transitioned to the common tongue. "Felled by the closest of allies." Hel pointed to the comatose silver-haired woman.

"You were felled by the closest ally of all. You gave yourself up in an attempt to save Talan."

Raine's jaw clenched, but she did not dispute this version of events, and Hel continued. The third line was illuminated, then translated in glowing letters.

"Carries into death without dying."

Hel paused. "And here you are, in the Underworld, the land of the dead, amongst death itself, and yet you still live."

This realization pierced Raine like an ice-cold needle through her heart. She had not considered the prophecy in that light, nor given it any connection to her current situation.

Hel waved the hand again, and yet another line illuminated and translated, which she read aloud.

"That which saves all worlds."

"And how have I saved any worlds?" Raine said, her bitterness even more pronounced. "I have saved nothing during my stay here."

"Oh, but you have," Hel said. "You see, the instant you were taken from that battlefield in Arianthem, I withdrew all of the Hyr'rok'kin from the mortal realm. The Veil has been emptied. I have not ventured one foray against the borders of Ásgarðr. I have not once left the Underworld to battle against any realm, content within my land for the first time in eons."

Raine sought to process this improbability, nay, this impossibility, that her presence at Hel's side had stayed the hand of the Goddess against her enemies, had protected the helpless in the mortal realm from her fiendish creations.

"You withdrew the Hyr'rok'kin from Arianthem?" Raine said uncertainly.

"I did. There was no battle after you leaped into my portal. I told the mortals to stay out of the Empty Land, stay clear of the Veil and Nifelheim, and that they would be troubled no more. I ordered my army of a million Hyr'rok'kin to stand down, and they marched back across the desert. There was no war, not even one death on the battlefield that day. And not one Hyr'rok'kin has passed into the mortal realm since."

This was too much for Raine to absorb. As much as she had tried to avoid thinking of her friends, thoughts of their demise had tortured her. She had visions of the destruction of her homeland, and the idea that it was still exactly the same, verdant and green, continuing on peacefully as if nothing had happened, was too much for her to comprehend. She stared dumbly at the glowing text on the wall.

"And so now, my love," Hel said, "would you like to see the final line of the prophecy?"

Raine stared as the symbols of the final line illuminated and began to glow. She could not breathe as Hel began to read the prophecy in its entirety.

"The Dragon's Lover, felled by the closest of allies, carries into death without dying, that which saves all worlds." Hel paused, waved her hand, and the final line translated itself into the common tongue.

"And whose destiny it is to be The Consort of the Queen of the Underworld."

Raine sat down heavily on the bench behind her, the bench she had sat on so many times before, pondering the massive curtains, never knowing that her lover was right behind her. She wanted to scream denials, to shout rejections, to declare it a lie and a falsehood, but in the end, she said nothing, because she knew in her heart that the translation was correct.

"Raine."

The whispered name was jarring to Raine, for she was not certain the Goddess had ever addressed her so before.

"You will be my Consort," she said softly, her emerald eyes glittering in her exquisitely beautiful face. The harshness of her words was an utter contrast to how gently they were spoken. "You have no choice, and no say. It is your destiny."

Hel left the room, and Raine leaned back against the amber block behind her, pressing against her lover's prison in anguish while she gazed up at the wall that spelled out her eternal damnation.

Hours passed, and Raine had moved only once. After staring at the words of the prophecy, she finally repositioned herself on the opposite bench so that she could look up at her love. Her eyes caressed those lovely, regal features. She ached to be so near her beloved, yet unable to touch her or speak to her. She worried for Weynild's condition, fearful that she could not maintain her stasis against that poisonous resin from that abomination in the garden. Tears flowed from her eyes, dried, then flowed again.

Hel came up from court and stood in the doorway, observing that her captive had barely moved.

"Come to bed."

Raine stared dumbly forward. Hel's words were not a request, but nor were they a command. They were more a statement of inevitability. Raine could hear the dragon's words in her head, the conversation they had in what now seemed lifetimes ago.

"I will not allow you to hate the part of you I so dearly love," Weynild's voice said. "Hel can force physical pleasure from you, but she cannot take your love. That belongs to me."

And Raine could hear her own response to her lover's avowal, to Weynild's insistence that she would not force her to move forward.

"If this ends as you say it will, I will endure anything."

Raine got to her feet and followed the Goddess from the room. She undressed under Hel's appreciative gaze and climbed into the massive bed. Hel spent hours exploring every inch of her body, as if laying claim to her anew, taking inventory of a new possession, then brought her to the gentlest, most sustained, most unrelenting climax yet, the act infused with Raine's melancholy and hopelessness, and driven by Hel's sense of entitlement to an inevitable prerogative. Raine fell asleep, the coldness of her cheek pressed against the shoulder of the Goddess.

Hel idly toyed with her captive's hair as the Arlanian slept. This moment, the one she had imagined over and over, had gone much as planned. The revelation of Talan's imprisonment and the final line of the prophecy had unfolded flawlessly. She was glad that Talan was now uncovered, if for no other reason than she enjoyed looking at her. Even now, she could see her immobilized ex-lover from her position in the bed, admire those elegant features and those golden eyes, appreciate the firm breasts pushed upward by that dragonscale armor, observe all of these lovely characteristics even as she ran her fingers through the hair of the dragon's lover.

Hel turned her attention to the one who slept curled against her, examining those perfect chiseled features, the long dark eyelashes that brushed those high cheek bones, the lips that even now caused desire to stir within the Goddess. The feel of that soft, silky skin pressed against her own sent a shiver of delight down her spine, and she buried her face in that fair hair, breathing deeply of the heavenly scent that was both a blessing and a curse to all Arlanians. She lay back on her black satin pillows, arching her back so that her breasts pointed high to the night sky, thinking that truly, the day's events had unfolded with perfection.

Chapter 21

The Queen of the Ha'kan sat uneasily about her own council table. She was flanked by her staff, Senta, Gimle, and Astrid. Her daughter and her staff were present, Dallan, Rika, Lifa, and Kara. Skye sat next to Dallan with her second-in-command and childhood friend, Torsten. The Ancient Dragon, Kylan, sat in her exquisite human form, flanked by the dark beauties that were her liege's children, Idonea and Drakar. Fortuitously, an envoy from the empire had just arrived in the form of the Knight Commander Nerthus, who had carried on a lengthy affair with Idonea and sought any excuse to see her. Y'arren sat with Elyara and her attendants, all who had somber looks on their faces.

"Y'arren," the Queen began, "I have never seen you so solemn. Please don't keep us in suspense any longer. Tell us your news."

"Forgive me, your Majesty," Y'arren said, her countenance filled with a sad wisdom. "I just wanted to ensure that Kiren's translation was correct. I will forward it to your First Scholar for review as well, but I am confident enough now to share it with you."

"Translation?" Halla said. "Kiren was able to translate the final line of the prophecy?"

"She was." Y'arren paused. "But it was not what we thought it was." She held out her hand and Elyara passed her the scroll. Y'arren began reading.

"The Dragon's Lover, felled by the closest of allies, carries into death without dying, that which saves all worlds." Y'arren took a deep breath.

"And whose destiny it is to be The Consort of the Queen of the Underworld."

There were gasps and exclamations of disbelief about the room. Drakar leaped to his feet.

"That can't be true."

Skye was also on her feet. "There must be some mistake!"

"I wish that there were," Y'arren said sadly, "and as I said, I will impose upon the Ha'kan scholars to check Kiren's work. But neither I nor my sages have found fault with her translation."

"But what of the other parts of the prophecy?" Idonea demanded. "They have yet to come true."

Y'arren did not respond, simply gazed across the table with her ancient wisdom. And all were left to ponder the events that had occurred thus far. Raine was undoubtedly the Dragon's Lover. She had been captured going to Talan's aid. And from what Fenrir relayed and Skye felt first-hand, Raine walked in the land of dead while still among the living.

Halla considered the lasting peace that had descended upon Arianthem since Raine had been captured, and the harmony, when viewed in this light, left a bitter taste in her mouth. Fenrir's troubled speculation on Hel's elevation of Raine only seemed to confirm the unbearable truth of the translation.

"It appears," Y'arren said, summarizing all their thoughts into her own self-recrimination, "that all of these years I was wrong. This is not a prophecy, but a curse."

Chapter 22

The clothes the handmaidens brought forward were different, and Raine eyed them with unease. They had a distinct cut and were far more formal than her usual Arlanian clothes. The Arlanian style was present in their design, that was apparent, but they also shared some of the features of Hel's flowing robes. The embroidery was similar, and the sash that went across her body from her right shoulder to her left hip was the same violet color as the hem and edging on Hel's mantle. They possessed their own malevolent style, and in short, the outfit looked very much a complement to Hel's royal raiment.

"What are these clothes?"

Feray adjusted the sash and the bottom of the jacket, although really, the adjustment was unnecessary. The Arlanian wore the uniform to perfection.

"This," Feray said, taking a step back to admire her work, "is the clothing worn only by the Royal Consort."

It was as Raine feared. Today would be the day that Hel would present her to the court as her chosen companion, her victory prize. Raine chafed at all the meanings in the title "consort," for in the mortal realm, it meant the spouse of the reigning monarch. She had only one wife, Raine thought grimly, and she was encased in amber in a state of hibernation.

Feray was finished with her ministrations and deemed her appearance fit.

"Come."

Raine took one last look into the shrine, one last glimpse of her love, then followed Feray out onto the balcony.

As soon as she appeared, the Great Hall fell into silence. Hel glanced up, examining the Arlanian's appearance, and a slow smile curved about her face. The mortal looked as stunning in that outfit as she had expected.

Raine squared her shoulders and began stalking down the stairs, requiring Feray to scramble to keep up with her. Faen stood at the bottom of the stairs, having acquired, in his opinion, the most odious task of the day. As soon as Raine approached, he went to one knee, an example for all others to follow lest there be any confusion as to the meaning of the mortal's garb. He looked up to see the look of triumph on the Arlanian's face, the smug superiority he knew would be there, and he was surprised that her expression was the same as it had always been. There was no supercilious or haughty air about her, merely the same moody disinterest she had always displayed towards him and every other creature in the Underworld. He felt an odd sense of relief, and an even more foreign emotion that he could only surmise might be respect.

Raine moved through the throng as quickly as possible, valuing none of the pomp and circumstance that attended her arrival. A vision of her and Weynild arriving at the Ceremony of Assumption in the land of the Alfar flitted through her mind, a trek she had taken far more leisurely on the arm of her love. She pushed the memory away forcefully. The only thing that had kept her sane was mentally separating her previous life with her current experience, and that was going to be so much more difficult now that she knew her love was here. She stalked up the stairs, stopping before Hel and bowing from the waist. Hel extended her hand, and Raine hesitated only briefly before she took the hand and kissed it as expected. She then took her place at Hel's side, staring out at the court and seeing nothing.

If asked, Raine could not have recounted any of the events or procedures of that morning. She simply sat, her mind a blank state, as the hours ticked by. The presentations began, and Raine did not see the various dignitaries and nobles that came to offer their salutations to the Queen, and to proffer their acknowledgements to her as well. She did not even see one who stood at the bottom of the stairs, a troubled look on his face as he examined her clothing, and it was not until Feray plucked her sleeve that she turned her attention towards him.

It was Fenrir, again in his human form, standing at the bottom of the stairs. His expression matched the torment inside of her, and a muscle in her jaw jumped as she clenched her teeth. The distress on his countenance, based upon the full understanding of her position, was evident to all. He now comprehended all of Hel's previous actions, her deference to Raine and her open regard for the mortal. It might as well have had nothing to do with Raine, for Hel would allow none to denigrate her Consort, for to denigrate her Consort would be to denigrate her. Hel had raised up Raine simply because Raine was now a reflection on her.

Raine glanced to Hel and it sufficed as a request. She would no longer demand public submission from her. In magnanimity towards her chosen one, she nodded her approval, and Raine stood and started down the stairs. Fenrir's glowing eyes rested on her clothing as she approached, his angry scrutiny expressing all.

The two just stood looking at one another, and Raine struggled to control her emotions. The hushed attention of everyone in the great hall was upon them.

"Is it true?" Raine said at last.

"Is what true?"

"Is it true that Hel has withdrawn all the Hyr'rok'kin from the Arianthem?"

"Yes," Fenrir said. He realized Raine knew nothing of the events of the mortal realm. "The Hyr'rok'kin withdrew the day that you were brought here."

This seemingly positive news caused a disquiet in Raine that was baffling to Fenrir. The Scinterian was engaged in some inner struggle that was reflected in the working of her jaw, the distant sadness in her eyes, the rising in her chest as she took a deep breath, and then the straightening of her spine as she stiffened with resolve.

"Then take a message to my friends."

Fenrir looked uneasily to his sister, for she was watching them intently as Raine continued.

"Tell them not to attempt to rescue me. Tell them to leave me to my fate."

Fenrir's heart fell and Hel leaned back in ultimate satisfaction. Raine merely turned on her heel, unable to bear the proximity of another whom she loved and could not touch. She strode back up the stairs, taking them two at a time, and sat down in her place on the left side of the throne.

Fenrir held his sister's gaze for a very long time, then he, too, spun about on his heel and left the throne room.

Chapter 23

Although Nerthus had meant to spend several days in the Ha'kan capital, her contrived visit had been cut short by the authentic crisis that had arisen. She had had spent only a single night with Idonea, and in contrast to their usual passionate encounters, the formidable, gruff Knight Commander had spent the twilight hours simply holding the raven-haired mage as Idonea fluctuated between tears and a wretched silence. Nerthus had hugged her at length early in the morning, then set back out to carry word of the new development to her Empress as quickly as possible.

So it was with some surprise that Aesa greeted her Knight Commander in a matter of days when her return was not expected for weeks. Bristol, too, was informed of Nerthus' arrival, and because little would pull his peer from her infatuation with Idonea, he knew her return could not be good news. He joined Aesa, who shuttled her great-grandchildren away with a servant, leaving only Malron'a hovering in the background with the two Knight Commanders and the Empress.

"Something has happened?" Aesa said, cutting right to the matter. Nerthus appreciated the straight-forwardness of the new Empress, having grown weary of the oily and officious, indirect, and time-wasting manner of the deposed Emperor.

"Yes," Nerthus said. "No sooner had I arrived in Haldis when Y'arren, the ancient seer of the wood elves, received word from the Alfar. The Directorate's young companion, the Lady Storr, succeeded in translating an ancient text that seems to refer to Raine."

"You speak of the prophecy regarding the Dragon's Lover," Malron'a said, coming forward from the shadows. She, too, was a seer, albeit of a much darker nature than Y'arren.

Aesa was somewhat familiar with the prophecy, but not entirely. Malron'a filled in the gaps in her knowledge.

"The Dragon's Lover, felled by the closest of allies, carries into death without dying, that which saves all worlds." Malron'a paused, addressing Nerthus. "But there was a final line, was there not? One that had proven too difficult to translate."

Nerthus nodded, her ruddy cheeks flushed with all the emotions the final line had stirred. "The Lady Storr believes the last line is, 'and whose destiny it is to be the Consort of the Queen of the Underworld.'"

Aesa's pale hand came up to cover her mouth. "Referring to Raine?" she said. "Raine is to be Hel's Consort?"

Nerthus nodded, her anger and disgust at the words palpable.

"That is not possible!" Bristol said, his own fury exploding. "That is just not possible!"

Malron'a ruminated on the words, calmer than Bristol, but no less moved. "Hel's Consort," she murmured, "that would be much like our dark Mistress."

Vampyr, and particularly those of the Shadow Guild, revered and worshipped Hel. Malron'a, whose real name was unknown to but a few, had a considerable affinity towards the Goddess of the Underworld. She had seen inklings of this fate, but it had not been clear. If this was Raine's destiny, then even she pitied her. "Then it was as much a curse as a prophecy."

"That's what Y'arren said."

"And so what do we do?" Aesa asked. "What is the plan now? We've been preparing troops to march across the Empty Land, but if there is no hope of victory, no chance to free Raine, then what do we do now?"

"Those who accompanied Raine to Hel's Gates before will go again," Bristol said. "None of us will leave her there."

"Bravery will not countermand fate," Malron'a said, her words cruel in their certainty.

Nerthus sought to interrupt the argument she saw developing.

"Y'arren is communing now, seeking a path forward. She told me she would send word as soon as possible."

"I am going to go train with the troops," Bristol said angrily, dismissing himself. "They will be ready to march across the Empty Land when Y'arren makes that call."

Malron'a watched the red-headed Knight Commander storm from the room, followed by his female counterpart. Yes, they would prepare the imperial army to march, march across a desert and into the face of annihilation, for it was certain Hel would not release that which fate had allowed her to claim as her own.

Chapter 24

Feyden sat in the library, rubbing his chin with his hands. Lorifal, his stout figure looking as if it might crush the delicate chair he sat upon, made odd faces as he ran his tongue along his teeth, his mouth closed. He did this when perplexed, and it always twisted his face into amazing contortions. Dagna stared down at the map that they had worked so hard on, having already committed it to memory. They sat alone amongst the walls of books.

"The translation has been confirmed," Feyden said, "both by the wood elf sages and the Ha'kan scholars."

The trio fell back into silence, accompanied by Lorifal's facial gymnastics and Feyden's rubbing of his chin.

"We will still go, of course," Feyden said.

"Aye," Lorifal said. They both looked to Dagna, who had not responded.

"What?" she said, roused from her reverie. "Of course we will, that goes without saying. I'm not as spry as I once was, but I'm still up for a fight."

"And Elyara?" Feyden prompted.

"I have never known her to go against Y'arren's wishes," Dagna said, "but I believe in this case, she will, if it comes to that."

"And Idonea," Lorifal began, then stopped himself. "Well again, that goes without saying. The lass will not leave her mother or Raine there. And I don't believe that Bristol will abandon our cause, either."

"So regardless of what the nations decide," Feyden said, "we are committed to moving forward, the six of us?"

"Yes," Lorifal said. "And I'm guessing that little firebrand of a Tavinter, Skye, the one who is connected to Raine, will not let us go without her, either."

Feyden nodded his agreement. "So even without Gunnar, with Skye we will still be seven, and once Raine is rescued, we will be eight. I'm guessing that Talan's son, and perhaps even the other Ancient Dragon, Kylan, will also accompany us, so we will have two dragons instead of just one."

"And once Talan is rescued," Dagna said, "we will have three."

None commented on how ridiculous their unspoken assumptions were, that they could even reach the Underworld, let alone infiltrate it to rescue Talan and Raine, then escape. They ignored the ridiculously small number of their proposed party, concentrating instead on its symbolic parallels to their previous journey, the similarity in numbers that was ultimately meaningless. And truthfully, not a one thought they would survive or succeed in their quest, but not a one of them was unwilling to try.

Chapter 25

Y'arren sat in the Queen's inner forum, gathered around the fire pit at its center. She was surrounded by the Ha'kan royalty and staff who sat on the cushioned seats around her, along with Idonea and Elyara. Drakar and Kylan stood, leaning against the pillars behind the seating area, and Skye moved restlessly about in the shadows.

"Do you have any more insight?" Queen Halla asked.

Y'arren was filled with an unusual uncertainty. "Isleif's plan, as brilliant as it was, did not account for this. We always assumed the final line of the prophecy foretold some great promise, that it would follow in the vein of the first lines."

"This doesn't change anything," Skye said, moving about the room. "It doesn't change a thing."

But she could see in the expressions of those surrounding her that it did indeed change things. Even Y'arren was dismayed by the words of the prophecy, words whose meaning she still couldn't grasp in their entirety.

"I have no doubt of your bravery," Y'arren said, "and of the bravery of all the peoples of Arianthem. I have not seen such unity of purpose since the Great War. But it is one thing to battle Hyr'rok'kin, demons, and the gods themselves; it is another to fight against the monolith of fate."

"Raine told me that fate is what you make it," Skye said, "if she said that once, she said it a dozen times."

"Yes," Idonea said quietly, "she told me that she would make her own destiny."

"She said that?" Y'arren asked. "In exactly those words?"

"Yes," Idonea said, "on many occasions. It always seemed to bring her comfort."

Y'arren mulled the words. There was nothing remarkable in them, she herself had heard Raine speak them. But in light of the current revelations, perhaps they had a deeper meaning. She would have to meditate upon them, to see if perhaps there was something profound there that she had missed.

"I do not have a clear path for us forward," Y'arren said, "so I suggest that everyone just continue to prepare as they have."

Skye did not wait, but strode out of the room to return to her training. Y'arren sighed, for the young Tavinter was becoming very headstrong, and without Raine's calming presence, more than a little reckless. The wise elf looked to the Ha'kan First General, who also was a calm, authoritative figure to Skye. Senta nodded her understanding and rose to seek out her First Ranger.

Y'arren returned to her thoughts, and as all quietly dismissed themselves, she was also aware of the meaningful look that passed between her apprentice and the dragon's daughter. She had no doubt that the comrades from the first quest, the bard, the knight, the dwarf, the mage, and the two elves, would all be returning to the Gates of the Underworld, regardless of the opinions or actions of anyone else in the world.

Chapter 26

The dim light was slightly brighter than its darkest state, giving Raine the subtle indication of daytime in the underground world. She was alone in the great bed, and all the despair caused by Fenrir's latest visit returned to her. She raised her head from the silk pillow. She could see Weynild from where she lay. The sight of her lover was enough to bring her to her feet and draw her into the shrine. She pressed her forehead against the cold, transparent prison, longing to touch her one and only love. The act made her ache, filled her with anguish. But for once her mourning was unaccompanied by the anxiety of discovery. Normally, she displayed little weakness or affection in the presence, or potential presence, of the Goddess, for there was no telling when Hel would appear. The Goddess moved about silently within her realm, at times passing through the land of the dead to materialize where she willed. This ability to move about undetected had created a constant wariness within Raine.

But that wariness was blunted today. Raine drew back from the block of amber, her brow wrinkled in thought. Something was different. She turned and re-entered the main bed chamber, looking about her, but she could see nothing out of the ordinary. She pulled on the clothes that had been laid out for her, then walked to the balcony leading to the throne room. The staircase was guarded by two great demons, barring her entrance into the hall, but that was not unusual. The throne room below was sparsely occupied, those few denizens present looking up to nod deferentially.

Raine returned to the bed chamber, ran her fingers through her hair, perplexed, then went to the terrace that led into the garden. It, too, was empty, save for the gardener who walked by in his dreamy ephemerality, oblivious to her presence. She stepped down onto the path, her brow still wrinkled in consternation, trying to figure out what was bothering her, what had changed. She trailed her fingers along the tops of the tall, florescent flowers, and the stems bent forward with her touch, then sprang back into position as she passed.

She stopped in front of the Tree of Death, that hated entity that had grown even more despised once Weynild's confinement was revealed. Her anguish returned and the sight of the glowing sap infuriated her, filled her with rage that this was the substance that had captured and imprisoned her dragon. Her fists clenched. Given the opportunity, she would destroy this monstrosity with her bare hands, but undoubtedly she would be stopped by the Goddess before she could even start.

Raine froze. That was it. That's what was different.

Hel was gone.

Raine was not certain how she knew it, other than she felt it, but to her it was as clear as the tree standing before her. Hel was not in the Underworld, and although Raine had no idea where she was, that mattered little to her. For this brief, shining moment, the shadow of the Goddess did not loom over her.

She strode back to the terrace, took the steps three at a time, and quietly pulled the two great doors that led to Hel's chambers closed. She grabbed the metal spade that had been left leaning against the new walls that surrounded the garden, the elaborate, heavy-duty gardening tool she had fantasized about using as a weapon. She spun it about on the palm of her hand, then shoved it through the heavy, engraved door handles. Now the only entrance to the garden was blocked, at least temporarily. Raine did not expect the doors to hold very long against the brute force of those demon guards.

She made her way back to the tree. Unfortunately, the spade was the only utensil left in the garden, so she had no tool with which to inflict damage. But as she stood before the malevolent, twisted trunk, she did not care. She would enjoy the pain this caused her.

She raised her bent arm, violently twisted her torso, and struck the tree such a blow with her elbow and forearm that a chunk flew from it as surely as had she struck it with a sledgehammer. Golden sap flowed downward like blood from a wound, and the reddish amber resin added to this symbolic imagery.

The Underworld shuddered.

Granted, it was a small shudder, a barely perceptible quake that left many wondering if they had imagined it. The demon guards glanced to one another, then shrugged their shoulders. Feray herself was seated at the time, and thought perhaps she had suffered a slight dizzy spell. Still, something caused her to get to her feet and to begin to search out the Arlanian.

Real blood flowed from Raine's forearm where the blow had split her skin, but she did not care. She raised her left arm, coiled her body in the same twisting posture, then unleashed another devastating strike with her other elbow. Another satisfying chunk of wood and bark flew off, and another bleed of sap and resin was opened. This strike was accompanied by another slight quake, making it clear Raine had not imagined the previous one. Although the quake was gratifying, she knew it would expose her actions. This did not give her pause, rather increased her urgency. She took a stance, then spun about on her planted foot, and delivered the devastating kick for which the Scinterian were feared. The sharp, leading edge of her shin cut through the wood as if it were an axe, causing damage to both the leg and the tree, but far more to the latter. This blow caused a perceptible rumble as her blood mingled with the golden sap of the tree.

Feray reached the doors to the garden as the ground distinctively shook for the first time. She saw with dismay that they were shut, and when she pulled to open them, was stopped by something jammed through the door handles on the other side. She peered through the small crack and saw the Arlanian covered in blood and glowing with sap.

"Get in here," she commanded, and the demon guards appeared. The intermittent rumbling was beginning to unnerve them, and they readily obeyed the handmaiden. Faen also appeared, having correctly deduced it was likely the mortal at the center of the disturbance.

"What is going on here?" he screeched as the two demons began struggling with the door. "What's happening?"

"The mortal is destroying the Tree of Death."

"Destroying—?" Faen could not even finish this impossible sentence, he shoved one of the massive demons, twice his size, out of the way so he could peer through the crack. He saw the Scinterian, blue and gold markings barely visible in the flurry of strikes she was unleashing on the tree, surrounded by a spray of sap and golden-red mist, at the far end of the garden. He shoved the demon guard back into place as the subterranean palace shook once more.

"Get this open!" he screamed.

The demon guards began struggling with the door to the degree that Raine could now hear them. This did not deter her actions, rather she increased her speed, the damage to herself and the tree growing accordingly. But although the tree was hemorrhaging sap and resin, it was not enough. She was running out of time, and she was not going to be able to destroy the abomination.

She stopped, breathing hard, oblivious to the blood running from every limb. Her anger had not lessened at all, rather was a seething river that flowed outward, desiring to destroy the garden with a tidal wave of rage. She did not know if she was capable of doing what she was about to do, truly, did not know if anyone was capable of it. But she was going to try.

She stepped toward the tree, put her arms around its massive trunk, placed her feet slightly wider than her shoulders, then squatted down. The circumference of the tree was such that her arms barely reached halfway on either side, but it did not matter as she tensed every muscle in her body and began to lift.

"What is she doing?" Faen said. He could barely make out the scene on the other side of the doors, but the demon guards had widened the gap and were close to dislodging or snapping the garden tool blocking their path. Apparently the mortal had completely lost her mind, because it looked as if she were trying to uproot the tree. This momentarily comforted him, because at least she had stopped damaging two of Hel's greatest prizes: the tree and herself. But his relief was short-lived as the ground began a low, sustained rumbling and the walls around him began to shake.

Feray had not even Faen's short relief. She had watched the mortal with growing apprehension, startled at the amount of damage she was inflicting on the tree. So when Raine took the position to uproot the monstrosity, Feray felt only alarm. She was not surprised when Raine slowly began to stand upright, her arms still wrapped around the tree.

Raine was aware of none of this. Every muscle in her body was corded, every ligament stood out in bold relief, every tendon was strained to its breaking point. Her face was a study in concentration, the stress evident in the tension in her jaw, but her expression was calm. Her pale blue eyes glowed with a preternatural light. Slowly, the tree began to rise, the roots began to move, the dirt beneath her feet shifted, and the Underworld again shuddered as something it could not comprehend began to happen.

"Get in there!" Faen shrieked as the spade finally broke and the doors flew open. The demon guards galloped across the garden, pikes held before them, but they slowed in disbelief as the Tree of Death came slowly free from the earth, its roots dangling above the black soil which had nourished it. The mortal was dwarfed by the enormous trunk she held, leaning back to balance the massive weight. Sap flowed outward from the hole in the ground left by the violent extraction. This river of sap was unlike any normal tree, for it bled from the hole as if its heart had been ripped out. Raine could not hold the tree any longer and released it, barely managing to stagger out of its way as the gigantic trunk began to fall sideways. It crashed downward, landing partly on the garden grounds and partly on the wall that had been erected to keep out the darkness.

Raine could not even stand. She wavered, stumbled, then fell to her knees in exhaustion. She would have pitched forward onto her face were her forehead not suddenly leaning against the thigh of the Goddess, who had materialized right in front of her.

Complete silence fell on the garden. Those who had been drawn by the rumbling, the commotion, and the gigantic thud of the tree trunk cowered in the doorway, peering over one another. Faen shrunk away from the black outline of the Goddess. Feray simply steeled herself, resolution on her features. The demon guards shriveled before their Queen.

Hel examined the fallen tree, her face expressionless. Her silent inventory of the damage seemed to go on forever, endless to those awaiting their fate. Raine was not one of these, for she was barely conscious, leaning against the Goddess, still on her knees. Hel turned her scrutiny to the prisoner at her feet, again silently inventorying the damage. Both arms and both legs were injured, sustaining wounds that made it appear the mortal had tried to beat the tree to death. Hel's perusal returned to the trunk of the tree as her hand absently stroked Raine's hair. It looked as if the attempt had been partially successful. The tree bore cuts and gouges about its lower extremity, covered in both sap and blood. She finally turned her emerald gaze to the roots, the exposed, twisted branches that somehow had been ripped free from the earth.

Hel let out a great sigh, reached down, grasped Raine by the collar, and lifted her clean off the ground. She gathered the limbs into position to carry her, propped Raine's head on her shoulder, and turned about. All those cowering in the doorway fled like rats, flitting away into the darkness. Both Feray and Faen stood with their heads bowed, and the demon guards recoiled as their Mistress passed.

But Hel did not look at any of them as she walked with her consort in her arms, lost in thought. She carried her captive up the stairs, then to the bed where she placed the prone figure in the sheets.

"Tend to her wounds," she said, and all the handmaidens jumped to comply, grateful for the strange, distracted air of their Mistress.

Hel returned to the garden, again passing Faen and Feray without reaction, and Feray had the presence of mind to wave the demon guards away. Hel stopped before the fallen tree, next to a transparent, flickering figure who leaned over the disaster in an attitude of dismay. Hel herself turned transparent, at least to the eyes of Faen and Feray, as she entered the realm of the dead.

The gardener, on the other hand, solidified and filled with color and form, at least in Hel's view. His dismay was even more evident as he muttered to himself about the calamity in front of him.

"Is it salvageable?" Hel asked.

"What?" the gardener sputtered, startled. He was not used to being spoken to, or even acknowledged. Hel ignored the gardener's informality because he was completely insane. The only coherent conversation he was capable of involved gardening, a skill in which he was without equal.

"Is it salvageable?" Hel repeated.

"No, no, not a bit," the gardener muttered. "Quite impossible. Too much damage. Who could have done such a thing?"

Hel frowned, but the gardener continued muttering to himself.

"Good thing, those saplings, good thing."

"What saplings?"

"What?" the gardener said, spinning around as if Hel had just appeared.

"The saplings?" Hel said, one fine eyebrow arching upward.

"Ah, yes," the gardener said, pleased with the subject and wondering how this lovely lady knew of it. "The saplings. Took the liberty of growing a few more of these, maybe an even better stock."

"How many more?"

"Three of four, maybe twenty."

"Maybe twenty?" Hel asked.

"No, no," the gardener said, shaking his head. "Who told you that? I have at least thirty."

A slow smile curved about Hel's features. "Look at me," she commanded.

The gardener finally made eye-contact with Hel and recognized his Mistress. He trembled. How long had she been standing here?

"The saplings, I want you to plant all thirty of them. I want an orchard of these trees."

The gardener beamed with pleasure, a maniacal look in his eye. "As you wish, your Majesty."

Hel settled onto her chaise throne next to the bed. The mortal had been cleaned and now had bandages on all four limbs. She slept restlessly, thrashing about, then wincing in her sleep at the pain the movement caused her. She was no less desirable for her battered and unconscious state, and had Hel been in the mood, she probably would have crawled into bed next to the Arlanian, pressed up against her skin-to-skin, then pleasured herself to satisfaction.

But Hel was not in that mood right now. Instead, she sat with her fingers tented, tapping the apex against her lips. It did not seem possible that this small, vulnerable creature lying in her bed had destroyed the Tree of Death. It did not seem possible that this mortal, Scinterian or not, was capable of uprooting that monstrous tree. Even the demons who had worked on it night-and-day, trying to fashion the hardened resin into twine, then rope, then chain, had been able to do little more than puncture it in strategic places to obtain the desired material. Many had died in the quest to create the substance from the sap that now entombed Talan.

Hel leaned back, her eyes still on her unconscious lover. Although she had no doubts as to her own power, she felt there were many in the pantheon who could not have accomplished what this Arlanian did today. And this was the great question that had blunted her anger and distracted her from administering punishment.

How had this mortal accomplished something that many of the gods could not?

Chapter 27

Idonea left Haldis by a side gate, quietly informing the guards she was going to go for a walk in the surrounding countryside. They graciously offered her accompaniment, as much to enjoy the company of the lovely mage as to protect her, an offer Idonea just as graciously declined.

She held in her hand a message, one that had simply appeared in her room, one without a courier or any obvious means of delivery. Idonea had only the slightest hint of the message's author when Rika commented that she thought she had seen a dog on the terrace.

And now she made her way through the forest, unthreatened by even the most dangerous of beasts, heading toward the requested rendezvous. Animals had a way of sensing what was prey and what was predator, and the one walking through their territory was certainly not prey. The fact that she was accompanied by wolves, unseen but nearby, was even further deterrent.

It was not long before Idonea sensed the presence of the one who had summoned her, and when Fenrir appeared before her, she gave him a deep curtsy.

"That is not necessary. You are as much Raine's daughter as Talan's, which makes you my equal."

"I don't believe I am your equal, Fenrir. But I am grateful for the honor you extend to me."

"Honors that I extend do not come with strings attached."

Idonea knew to what he referred. "You speak of your sister. We translated the final line of the prophecy, and it appears your concern was valid. She did indeed have an ulterior motive, to make Raine her Consort."

"Yes," Fenrir said. "Hel would require her Consort to be venerated, so her elevation of Raine was as much for herself as it was for the Scinterian."

"I would argue that it was entirely for herself," Idonea said bitterly.

"And you would get little argument from me," Fenrir said, "although Hel does treat her so curiously."

"You have seen her again?" Idonea asked, keying on his melancholy tone.

"Yes. She now wears the raiment of the Consort, so it has been officially declared, at least in the Underworld."

"Where else would it be declared?" Idonea asked, her eyes narrowing.

"That is one of the reasons I asked you to speak with me. It has been brought to my attention that Hel has visited Ásgarðr of late, and upon more than one occasion."

"What purpose would Hel have in visiting the heavenly city?"

"I'm not certain. She hasn't been there for eons, a mutual disenchantment between her and the rest of the pantheon."

Fenrir could see that Idonea did not understand the politics he was trying to suggest. "I should explain. Contrary to what mortals believe, the Underworld was not given to Hel as a punishment, but as a reward. It is a position of unmatched power and responsibility."

"And why was it given to Hel?"

"Loki, our father, was always one of the Allfather's favorites, and Hel is his favorite grandchild."

"Really?" Idonea said, thinking far less of the Allfather.

"Yes, and now it appears she is back in his good graces since she has been on her best behavior."

"And when did this good behavior start?" Idonea asked sarcastically.

"When do you think?" Fenrir responded.

"When Raine was taken."

"Yes, what the gods consider good behavior and what we would consider good behavior are two different things. Hel has kept her Hyr'rok'kin from the mortal realm, has stopped her endless forays against the borders of other realms, and in short, has done everything to gain in favor with her grandfather."

"Even though she has kidnapped my mother and Raine to do so."

"The gods care little for such trifling details," Fenrir said, making it clear by his tone and expression that he did not consider them trifling, and that he himself cared a great deal. "Raine also sent a message," he continued reluctantly, "one directed to all of her friends, but one I feel I should give only to you."

"What message?"

"She asked me if it was true that Hel had withdrawn the Hyr'rok'kin from Arianthem, and that there was no battle the day that she was taken. When I told her yes, I could tell by her face that she had not known. When I confirmed that these things were true, she said 'tell my friends not to attempt to rescue me. Tell them to leave me to my fate.'"

"So Hel has told her of the prophecy."

"It would seem so."

"So is that why you came?" Idonea asked angrily. "To talk us out of rescuing her? To leave my mother to some unknown fate?"

"Of course not," Fenrir said, his dark eyes glowering. "I would never abandon my friend."

"Then why are you here?"

"Because," Fenrir said, exasperated, "not everyone in Ásgarðr is as fond of Hel as the Allfather, and, for whatever reason, certain gods have been willing to slip me information on her comings and goings."

Understanding was beginning to dawn on Idonea.

"And if I know when my sister is absent from the Underworld," the wolf god continued, "the best time to mount an attack will be—"

Idonea finished for him.

"—when she's gone."

Chapter 28

The touch of the handmaidens awoke Raine. They were washing her wounds and rewrapping her bandages with great care. Hel sat on her throne, observing the ministrations of her servants, and her emerald eyes flicked to Raine as she stirred.

"Her wounds heal quickly," one handmaiden said.

"And cleanly," said a second.

The handmaidens often finished one another's sentences, and a thought would sometimes require the entire group before it could complete itself.

"When most in the Underworld don't at all," said a third.

"And they didn't even touch these pretty markings," said a fourth, caressing the Scinterian scars.

"That is enough," Feray said, clapping her hands. The handmaidens reluctantly obeyed, quitting the most pleasant duty assigned them. Feray tried to judge the mood of her Mistress at these improprieties, but Hel did not appear even to notice. Her focus had been entirely on the Arlanian since the moment she had returned, her vigil comparable to the one that she had undertaken when the mortal had first been captured in Nifelheim.

"Is there anything else you require?" Feray asked.

"No."

Feray bowed out of the room. The expected punishment had never come, not for her or Faen, nor for the guards. She wondered if the mortal herself would bear the brunt of Hel's anger, and almost felt pity for the

Arlanian.

Raine was silent in the bed, steadily returning the gaze of the Goddess.

"You will not," Hel began, "destroy anything else in my garden."

Raine recognized the manner of speaking. Punishment could come as a result of disobeying many things in the Underworld. Things that were understood, things that were implied, things that were written down somewhere. And then there were the things that came from Hel's mouth as direct commands. To disobey an explicit order from the Goddess was to risk annihilation, and Hel spoke the words as if obedience was not only expected, but a foregone conclusion. All that was required was for her to speak, and the thing was done.

Raine said nothing.

"And you will not damage yourself in such a way," Hel continued, nodding at the bandages, "again."

Raine still said nothing, and Hel merely sighed and stood up. She approached the bed, and it was with some consternation that Raine realized she could not move. The Goddess was restraining her, something she had done less and less of late.

"So many of my subjects are easy to discipline," Hel said, sitting down on the bed. "They respond to pain, to torture, to threats, to humiliation, even to the Membrane. But you," Hel said, resting her hand upon Raine's thigh. "You respond only to one thing."

The hand disappeared beneath the robe, stroked the inside of the thigh, and found what it was seeking. Raine muffled a cry, desperate to maintain any semblance of control, and closed her eyes against the sensation. Hel watched for the tell-tale signs that told her all resistance had vanished, and they were not long in appearing. She had only to thrust her fingers up inside that inviting warmth, begin a gentle circular motion with her thumb, and the nipples hardened, the lips parted, and the eyes opened, their violet depths filled with self-recrimination.

"Ah, that's better," Hel said as her hand continued its gentle work. "All I do is bring you pleasure, raise you up above all my subjects, and you return my generosity by destroying my garden."

Raine would not argue with her, not expound the endless list of grievances she had against the Goddess, not detail the infinite, hated things that she carried in her heart. She would only endure Hel's attentions, endure her own weakness, and keep her heart and mind separate from what was happening.

Hel had no designs on Raine's heart, but the mind would belong to her. "Oh, I don't think so," she said, and leaned down to kiss Raine with a passionate and prolonged probing. The connection had the desired effect, for Raine was no longer a passive recipient of pleasure, but actively returned the kiss. Hel murmured her own pleasure as she felt the quickening rhythm of the hips, and then the release between the legs as they surrendered to the thumb and fingers. There were times when Hel wanted to prolong the act, delay the gratification, and there were times when she wanted to bring climax quickly, affirming her mastery of the body beneath her hand. This was one of those times.

But Hel was not done, that much was clear as Raine sought to catch her breath and the Goddess stood and removed her robes. Raine did not want to look at the voluptuous curves, the beautiful breasts, the flat stomach and all that lie below. But her eyes sought out the demonic loveliness like an addict sought out the drug that would destroy her.

"I hope your injuries don't bother you too much," Hel said, rolling Raine over onto her stomach, then burying her face in her hair. "You have a long day ahead of you."

A spot of blood had seeped through on the forearm bandage, but that was the only sign of damage from the day's rigor. It really had been a day for the ages, Hel thought, and she could not recall ever having taken such pleasure in the discipline of another. Although her treatment of the Arlanian could hardly be called punishment, the marathon session was indeed punishing.

Her captive stirred, and Hel adjusted her position so that Raine's head was on her chest, but she could still look into the side room and see her other captive. Raine lifted her head, disoriented, and her eyes focused upon Hel and their intimate position. She followed Hel's gaze to the translucent amber prison, then lowered her head back down.

Hel toyed with Raine's hair, still admiring Talan in the adjacent room.

"Do you think she can see us?"

Raine's response was immediate. She turned her back to the Goddess. "There is no 'us.'"

Hel's reaction was just as immediate. She rolled Raine onto her back and pinned her so they were now face-to-face.

"Perhaps I should have been more clear," she said through gritted teeth. "What I meant to say is, do you think she can see you writhing beneath me, moaning, coming over and over and over again, as I climax on top of you?"

Raine stared up at the woman, her eyes blue, her tone even, and although her words were whispered, they were quite clear.

"For your sake, you'd better hope not."

Hel shoved her to the side in disgust, got up, and yanked on her robes. She strode from the room, knocking over a black vase which fell to the ground, shattering into a thousand pieces.

Raine pulled the sheets up around her neck, shivering. Her body temperature had dropped precipitously as Hel's fury had spiked. She rolled over onto her side, gazing at the silver-haired woman who stared out at nothing. Despite her cold and exhaustion, she gathered the sheets to her and got out of bed. She padded into the shrine, wrapped the sheets about her as best she could, then curled up on the floor next to the block of amber. She drifted off to sleep, unconcerned that she would be found, doubting that there was anything else she could do that would make Hel any angrier than she already was.

Chapter 29

If only there were more of our kind," Kylan said.

She sat in the Ha'kan royal garden, admiring Idonea's skill as she cast a number of spells. Drakar, too, admired his sister, for reasons beyond her skill.

"We had no choice but to kill those that sided with Volva," Drakar said.

"No," Kylan said, "I'm not talking about them. I have no qualms about killing the lesser of our kind. I wish that we had more Ancient Dragons."

"Well, you and my mother, not to mention Raine, have had your hand in their dwindling numbers."

"Don't make me clarify myself further, boy," Kylan said, "I meant more dragons of your mother's pedigree."

"Well, I have been attempting to plant my seed in almost everything that moves for years, with absolutely no luck."

"That is because you are, or at least will be, an Ancient Dragon. We are not very fertile."

"You have no children?" Drakar asked, for the first time realizing Kylan had never spoken of offspring.

"No," the dragon said, "like you, it's not for lack of trying. But I guess Ancient Dragons were meant to be rare. Speaking of which," Kylan said as something occurred to her, "you slept with Volva, did you not?"

"It is the first and only time in my life I have used protection," Drakar said, raising his hands. "The thought of accidently breeding with that witch turned my stomach."

"Good," Kylan said, relieved. But then the details piqued her interest. "And how exactly did you do that?"

"A nice little spell from my little sister, encasing the family jewels in an invisible barrier."

"She really is talented, isn't she?" Kylan said, her attention returning to Idonea.

"That she is," Drakar agreed, and Kylan cast him another glance. The boy's infatuation really was something to behold.

"Speaking of Volva," Kylan began, and Drakar immediately interrupted.

"Let's go kill her."

"What I was going to say," Kylan continued, "is now that I am healed and we are currently of little use here, perhaps we should go seek her out."

"And kill her."

"Volva will not fall as easily as Jörmung did," Kylan warned. "She is far more dangerous and would be a challenge even for your mother."

"Still, I think we should kill her."

Kylan sighed. "Yes, that would ultimately be the goal. To kill her. Or at least disable her enough so that she can't interfere in our plans. The problem is, she can sense me coming from miles away. The only way she and Jörmung were able to surprise your mother was Hel let them pass through Nifelheim."

"Even then, my mother was expecting them."

"Yes, but because your wise mother knew they were coming, not because she sensed them. But Volva will know that I am near, and I certainly can't cut through Hel's realm."

"I see," Drakar said. "This is a problem."

"I would not be surprised if Volva can sense you, too," Kylan said, "you are getting very near your maturity."

The comment filled Drakar with pride, causing him to puff out his chest in a juvenile display that instantly belied the compliment.

"Or not," Kylan said. A newcomer entered the garden, and the cool blue eyes settled on the fair-haired Tavinter. "Now that is a possibility."

"What is a possibility?"

"That youngster there, Skye. I have seen the spells she has been working on. They might serve to conceal a dragon."

"Do you think she can hide something that big?"

"I do," Kylan said, "and we could certainly test it out ahead of time. I
wonder if she would be interested?"

"Oh please," Drakar said, rolling his eyes. "I have seen the way she
looks at you. You need only thrust your breasts in her face and she will
follow you anywhere."

Kylan turned to him, taking a deep breath that caused her cleavage
to rise and drew Drakar's eyes magnetically to the soft mounds beneath his
nose.

"As will I," he admitted, "as will I."

"Good," Kylan said, releasing the breath. "I will ask her at first opportunity."

The ball of light winked out, perfectly controlled, and Skye wiped the
sweat from her brow. She sat down and leaned over to grab the small ce-
ramic jug that rested in the shadows of the bench. The cool water quenched
her thirst, and she poured a small amount in her cupped hand and patted
the back of her neck. The trail of liquid ran down her back beneath her
shirt, refreshing her further.

"You are getting much better."

Skye jumped to her feet as the gorgeous dark-haired woman in the
equally gorgeous blue gown approached.

"Thank you, your—," Skye paused, searching for a title. She was not
as polished as the Ha'kan and had no idea what to call the Ancient Dragon,
but some sort of honorific seemed necessary. "—your excellency," she finished lamely.

"Kylan is fine," the woman said with a smile and a twinkle in her eye.
She sat down on the bench and patted the spot next to her. "Come join me
for a minute."

Skye sat down next to her, certain that the dragon could hear her
heart pounding in her chest. Kylan possessed the same dark sensuality that
Talan did, those tendrils that seemed to snake out from the dragons and

wrap themselves about everyone and everything in the vicinity. Skye could feel the imaginary appendages coil about her, settle onto her with a pleasant weight that took her breath away.

"So," Kylan began, "can you explain to me the difference between your invisibility spell and the ephemeral spell?"

"Of course," Skye said, relieved to talk of a subject with which she was familiar. "The invisible spell renders an object, well, invisible. It can't be seen, but it's still there. You can feel its outlines. Here, like this." Skye picked up the jug once more and handed it to Kylan. She concentrated, and the jug disappeared.

"I can still feel its weight," Kylan said, hefting the invisible object.

"Yes," Skye said, waving her hand and making the jug reappear. "The jug could still be handled, picked up, dropped, even broken. It just can't be seen." Skye took the jug from Kylan's hands and set it on the bench between then. "But ephemeral is different."

Skye again waved her hand, and the jug again disappeared.

"Try to touch it."

Kylan reached out, but there was nothing there.

"Ephemeral makes the object, not only invisible, but untouchable as well. Careful," Skye said, moving Kylan's hand out of the way. The jug reappeared at her mental command. "I'm not sure what will happen if the jug returns when another object is occupying the same space, but I can't imagine it would be good."

"Fascinating," Kylan said. The Tavinter was as talented as Idonea said, wielding a form of light magic that she had never seen.

As if the thought of her had conjured her from thin air, Idonea appeared.

"And what are you two doing?"

"Not what you think, my love," Kylan said at the suggestive tone. She gave Skye a quick once-over that made her blush. "Although that is not out of the question for some time in the future. Anyway, Drakar and I were discussing a little side mission since the two of us seem relatively worthless at the moment."

"And does it involve a gold dragon?" Idonea asked.

"It does," Kylan confirmed. "Drakar and I thought we might seek out Volva, keep her from interfering in the larger plan."

"If the larger plan is even carried out."

"Come my love," Kylan said shrewdly, "even if all the races of Arianthem yield to the prophecy, you and your comrades will go on without them."

"As will I," Skye said. "I will not abandon Raine to the Underworld."

Idonea nodded, although she wondered if Skye knew what she was getting herself into. Then again, this youngster had already spent three years at war with the Ha'kan, had battled the sorceress Ingrid and won, and had thrived in a life of hardship and adversity that would have crushed most.

"You're going to have to get permission from your command to go with Kylan," Idonea reminded her.

"Right," Skye said, her enthusiasm and bravado wilting under this reminder.

Senta sat on the terrace with the Queen, Astrid, and Gimle, and the four were having morning tea as was their custom before each set out for their daily duties. She observed Skye approach from the adjacent terrace, accompanied by Idonea. The determined look on Skye's face, as well as her resolute posture, made Senta suppress a smile, but also made her wary. This was usually Skye's attitude when she was about to engage in something particularly reckless.

Skye stopped before Senta, bowed, then addressed her by her rank and title.

"First General."

Skye's excessive formality further heightened Senta's wariness, and caught the attention of the three other women at the table.

"Your Majesty, First Scholar, High Priestess," Skye said.

"Hello Skye," Queen Halla said.

"What can I do for you, First Ranger?" Senta said, both stern and sardonic.

Skye took a deep breath. "I would like to request a leave of absence for a few days."

Senta leaned back in her chair and clasped her hands, considering the request. "And what would be the purpose of this leave?"

Skye could make up any excuse, even say she was going to see her people in the woods for a few days, but she was a terrible liar. "Kylan has asked for my help."

"Kylan?" Senta said in surprise. A glance to Idonea confirmed the claim. "And what does Kylan need help with?"

Skye was trying to remain serious, but she could not hide the gleam that appeared in her eye.

"We're going dragon hunting."

"The gold dragon," Idonea said, stepping forward, "the one who was at the battlefield in the Empty Land, her name is Volva. She, Kylan, and my mother, are now the only Ancient Dragons left until my brother comes of age. She is dangerous to the people of Arianthem, and regardless of the path we take to move forward, her removal would benefit all."

Gimle considered these words. "What does Y'arren say?"

"She is still uncertain how to proceed given the prophecy, but she thinks this might be a chance for Skye to test her abilities in a controlled situation," Idonea said.

"Fighting an Ancient Dragon is hardly a controlled situation," Gimle murmured.

"Better an Ancient Dragon than the Goddess of the Underworld," Idonea said, "at least as a trial run."

"You're going to go by yourself?" Senta asked, turning back to Skye.

"Well, with Kylan and Drakar."

"I'm not even going," Idonea said. "This is one of those situations where the bare minimum is the best option. Stealth is needed above all. At least until the fight begins. Then what's needed is Kylan."

"I see," Senta said. "Then I will grant your leave of absence on one condition."

"What condition is that?" Skye asked.

"You must promise to return to us in one piece."

Chapter 30

kye rode on the back of the blue dragon, the thrill almost too much to comprehend. The cold wind blew through her hair and she leaned down to gain the heat from the dragon's body. Kylan had warned her to dress for the cold; now she understood why. A vapor trail outlined Drakar's body flying next to them, leaving ice particles in their wake. They were flying very high to avoid detection on the first part of their journey while they were still visible.

Despite the cold, the flight was glorious, and Skye was aware of the rare honor that was being bestowed on her. Few in all of history had been granted leave to ride a dragon, for they were intensely proud creatures. And even though Kylan granted this honor to her because she needed her help, Skye appreciated it all the same. She unconsciously stroked the soft, reptilian skin between the armored plating, then blushed at her impertinence.

Kylan felt the caress and smiled. Although sensual, it was not sexual, an unconscious gesture from one who lived and breathed as a part of the natural world. The girl's love for the Ha'kan must be great, because ones such as these usually never left the forest.

"You don't have to stop, but I must tell you, if you overstimulate me, I'll make you release any pressure you build."

Skye was now uncertain whether to stop or to use both hands. Dragons in human form were imposing, in dragon form they were terrifying. She put both hands back on the bony ridge she was using to hang on.

"Coward!" Drakar said, laughing.

"That's all right," Kylan said, "conserve your strength. We're going to need it in a little while."

Skye leaned back in the gap between two enormous spikes, the bony structures providing a saddle of sorts. The ground beneath them was beginning to slant upwards, gradually at first, but then more and more steeply. The air grew even colder and Skye shivered, as much from excitement as from the chill.

"We're getting close," Drakar rumbled. When he had pretended to ally himself with Volva, he had gained information on her various holds. After reviewing the locations on a map, Kylan had chosen the one she felt Volva would most likely be holed up in. It was an educated guess at best, but Drakar thought it was a good one.

"Yes," Kylan agreed. "If we move any closer, she will begin to sense me and our element of surprise will be lost." The enormous head of the blue dragon turned around and the pale blue eyes looked at Skye. "Are you ready?"

"I am," Skye said with confidence. Organic objects were more difficult than inanimate objects, but they had practiced for several days. Once Skye had overcome her initial trepidation about casting a spell on something so large, she was able to turn both Kylan and Drakar invisible, then ephemeral, then maintain the spell for quite some time. If things worked out the way they had planned, she would not have to maintain Drakar's spell for very long, and Kylan's only slightly longer.

Skye took a deep breath, focused her energy, and then released both. Both dragons and their rider disappeared.

A grin revealed a mouthful of translucent fangs on the formerly blue dragon. Kylan could see the transparent outlines of Drakar and Skye, and everything else in the world was transparent as well. When Skye had turned them merely invisible, they appeared translucent to one another, but the world around them was largely the same. When she used the more advanced spell of ephemerality, everything looked fluid and water-like. It took some practice navigating at first, for the spatial clues of light and shadow were greatly diminished, but once that hurdle was overcome, they could move about freely in the world, completely unseen and untouchable.

And hopefully undetectable to other magical creatures, Kylan mused, because she could now sense Volva in Felag Keep in front of them. That meant that her educated guess on Volva's location had been correct, and it also meant that, if the ephemeral spell did not cloak them completely, then Volva already knew they were coming. If the gold dragon was alerted to their presence, she would flee, and their long trek would be wasted. But they were still some ways off, and Volva's presence remained steady, so the two dragons flapped onward to their destination. Felag Keep appeared in the clouds ahead, perched on the side of a cliff, inaccessible other than to creatures of flight.

The two dragons circled overhead. There were no signs of alarm in the gigantic courtyard below. The castle was built to house dragons in their natural form, and the immensity of its size was apparent as a handful of lesser dragons perched on the parapets like birds. As expected, they were few, for Kylan and her allies had destroyed almost all who stood against Talan. What remained was a rag-tag group of reptiles still nursing their wounds.

Drakar looked to Kylan, and she nodded. He turned to Skye.

"When I give the signal," he said, then dove downward to the court-yard.

Skye watched the sleek dragon plummet. It was difficult to make out his form when he and the background looked so similar. Everything was just clear and fluid-like. But fortunately her eyes were keen and she saw his barrel-roll. She concentrated and released him from the spell.

Nothing changed, at least from her perspective. Drakar and every-thing else remained translucent. But his effect on the other translucent beings was pronounced. As the black dragon appeared in the sky above them, they scattered like a startled flock of pigeons. Seeing that he was only one, however, they regrouped and took chase, for Drakar was already fleeing across the tree-tops.

"Good boy," Kylan murmured. Drakar had wanted to fight, to go in with fire-breathing fury and destroy those who had dared stand against his mother, but Kylan had convinced him it would be better to act as a decoy. It was his job to lead away as many as he could, leaving Volva to Kylan. He was reluctant at first, for Kylan was still injured and Volva was at full-strength, for she had not even had to fight in the battle that had never happened. But Kylan had convinced him she would stand a better chance against Volva one-on-one than the two of them would stand against a multitude of dragons. And she did not want to strain the Tavinter to hide them for longer than necessary.

Kylan landed gracefully in the courtyard. Even this maneuver had taken some practice, for the dragons could pass right through things in their ephemeral form. But Skye had figured out that objects had to have a degree of solidity, even when the spell was cast, otherwise they never would have been able to flee the Hyr'rok'kin the first time she cast the spell. They would have just begun sinking into the ground, perhaps giving them a quicker trip to the Underworld than any of them expected. She had pondered this incongruity at length, then finally determined that the ground was solid because she expected it to be solid, and that this held true for other things as well, such as stairs and the terrace of the castle. It appeared there was a degree of belief in light magic that was wholly absent in dark magic, adding a multitude of dimensions to spells. Right now the terrace was solid enough for Kylan to land on simply because Skye wished it so.

She slid from Kylan's back, also landing on the transparent but solid-enough stone of the courtyard. The massive iron gate flickered fluidly. Although the spell rendered objects translucent, it did not render them entirely see-thru. Rather than looking through glass, it was like looking through thick, viscous fluid and little could be seen beyond immediate objects.

"You should be able to pass right through that gate," Skye whispered.

"I thought you said no one can hear us?" Kylan whispered back.

"They can't," Skye said, then realized she was still whispering. "They can't," she said in a more normal voice. She also straightened upright, realizing she was crouched down for no reason. "This takes a little getting used to."

"I see that," Kylan said, her irrepressible humor shining forth even in their tense situation. Skye blushed, and although color was absent in their world, somehow the dragon knew it. "Well," Kylan said, "let's do this."

Kylan took a deep breath and passed through the iron gate. Although they had practiced moving through objects, it was still unnerving. Skye crept along behind her, unable to shed her stealthy ways no matter how many times she reminded herself she couldn't be seen.

They moved through the castle and Skye marveled at its size. Kylan was enormous, only slightly smaller than Talan, and two of her girth could have passed one another in that hallway. A full regiment of Ha'kan could have stood in formation in the passageway. The rooms themselves were even larger, and Skye imagined the dragons lounging about as she peered through the gigantic doorways. It reminded her of a Tavinter folk tale of "the little people." She had been enamored with the idea of the tiny creatures interacting with normal-size objects, using a thimble as a bucket and a sewing needle as a sword. Right now, her sword felt a lot like that sewing needle.

Kylan seemed to know where she was going, moving unerringly into the castle, and Skye could only surmise that she could sense the other Ancient Dragon ahead of them. Drakar had done well, for he had drawn away all others and they came across no other of the lesser dragons. Finally, Skye began to hear a low rumbling that she had heard once before, when they had been on their journey to the Alfar Republic. Talan had slept out in the open, Raine curled about her sleeping form, and the rumble had been the sound of her breathing.

The gold dragon was indeed asleep, and even in her translucent state, her size was ominous. She was larger than Kylan.

"'Tis a pity you cannot affect objects while in this state," Kylan said, gazing at her sleeping enemy.

"That would be ideal," Skye admitted. But she was unable to cast any other spells while the ephemeral spell was active on herself. It seemed an either-or proposition. Nor was she able to physically affect other objects. Nothing could touch her, but neither could she touch anything else.

"Are you ready?"

Kylan nodded. "You stay hidden, but release the spell on me."

Skye took a deep breath, then released Kylan from ephemerality.

To Skye's view, nothing changed, but for Kylan, the room came into full relief. Volva twitched and began to stir, sensing the presence of her enemy. Kylan did not wait, but blasted her with frost from her lungs. The angled attack was devastating, the bitter cold blowing scales and plates from the gold dragon and leaving reddened, bloody flesh exposed.

Volva screamed and Skye covered her ears, fleeing to a corner. Although nothing could touch her, the sight of two Ancient Dragons fighting in such close quarters was terrifying. Skye concentrated on maintaining the spell on herself because the thrashing tails and flying furniture would have crushed her.

Volva attacked before she was even fully aware of her enemy. Kylan was engulfed in flame, facing the gold dragon full on. This greatly diminished the effect of the attack, for dragon scales were designed to repel frontal assaults, and even those from the side. That's why Kylan's initial attack had been so successful; she had taken advantage of the weakness to the rear without the normal protection of the tail.

"You bitch!" Volva shrieked.

Kylan did not waste breath on a retort, rather blew out another bitterly cold attack. Volva countered with fire, but Kylan's second attack was also effective, burning the exposed wounds with frostbite and causing the gold dragon to scream again. Skye could not imagine the fluctuating temperatures in the room, and had a greater appreciation for the Scinterians who had battled them. Volva's flame would have melted her and Kylan's frost would have frozen her solid. Either one would have killed her instantly.

Kylan whipped her tail around and the barbed spikes raked across Volva's face. Volva retreated out-of-range of the deadly appendage and let loose another funnel of fire. Kylan countered with frost and closed the distance between them, her great jaws snapping outward at Volva's wildly undulating neck. Kylan clearly had the upper hand and was pressing her advantage, slowly but surely cornering her adversary.

But something about Volva's retreat was bothering Skye. Perhaps it was Tavinter intuition that caused her to scan the area around the dragons. It was hard to see because the world was still the clear viscous fluid to her, but the trap became apparent when she looked hard enough.

"Look out!"

But Skye's warning went unheeded because it went unheard. Still within the ephemeral spell, Kylan could no more hear Skye than she could see her. Volva tripped the hidden switch and Kylan looked up just in time to see the boulders tumbling down upon her. The huge rocks struck her in the head, stunning her, then trapping her wings as she crumpled to the ground.

"I had saved this for Talan," Volva said, "just in case she ever escaped the clutches of Hel. But I'm happy to use it on you." She flicked another switch with her tail.

Skye looked up in horror as an enormous block of stone came tumbling down from the top of the tower. It was so massive it would crush Kylan, who was pinned by the smaller boulders. Skye did not think she had enough left in her to remove Kylan from the path of the falling stone, so she did the next best thing.

The stone disappeared.

Volva stared in disbelief as the massive block winked out of sight. Expecting to see the bloodied remains of her enemy smashed to bits, instead she was left staring at empty space. And beyond that empty space stood a small figure in the far corner of the room, hands raised as if admitting that she was the one who had just thwarted all her carefully laid plans.

Skye stared at the gold dragon, who was now visible in full color since she had released the spell on herself in order to cast the spell on the block of stone and make it pass through Kylan and the floor.

"You!" the dragon hissed.

Skye did not hesitate but fled through the door. The thud of the dragon in pursuit shook the castle walls and they shook more as Volva came through the doorway, taking out half the stone supports as she skidded around the corner. Skye used every bit of her Tavinter speed as she sprinted down the massive hallway, trying to gather her strength to cast a spell, knowing that the sewing needle at her side was useless.

She cringed as if she sensed an impending attack and darted behind a stone pillar as fire blasted down the passageway. She did not wait even a moment, but began sprinting down the blackened tiles toward the entrance, desperately trying to decide on a course of action. She might have just enough strength left to make herself ephemeral once more, but that would leave Kylan at the mercy of Volva. No, she really only had one option, and she was not even certain that she could do it, or if it would work. Her lungs burned as she ran towards the open gate, and she could feel the dragon right behind her. One last burst of speed put her through the opening…

And then the dragon screamed.

Skye stumbled and went to the ground, holding her ears against the awful noise. She crawled on all fours away from the dragon who was now thrashing about in agony. She pulled herself behind a stone bench, trembling as she looked over the top of it.

Volva was trapped by the iron gate that had not been open. In her pursuit, the path before her was clear and she assumed the gate was retracted upward. But Skye had used all that was left of her strength to make it ephemeral. She had hoped to kill the dragon, but Volva had nearly been on top of Skye when she sprinted through. When the gate materialized, it materialized across Volva's tail, severing, or nearly severing, the appendage.

Volva, in her agony and rage, finished the job as she pulled her bulk away from the iron gate and separated the tail. She thrashed about in torment once more, and Skye ducked down beneath the bench. But Volva wasn't looking for her any longer, and Drakar's distant roar of challenge removed any thought of remaining. The gold dragon staggered to the right, then awkwardly took flight, her aerodynamics completely compromised by the lack of a tail. She flapped in an ugly, cumbersome manner, and were it not for the steepness of the surrounding terrain, she might have plummeted to the ground. But she was able to glide down the incline, gaining no altitude, but escaping on the updrafts of the mountain air.

Drakar landed a few moments later to find the Tavinter sitting dumbly on the bench. She seemed in total shock, which was fitting given the amount of blood and damage in the courtyard.

"By the gods," he said, transforming to his human state, "what happened here?"

Skye looked up at the handsome young man. "We're going to have to figure out a way to open that gate."

They found Kylan still trapped beneath boulders. She was battered and bruised, as well as a little stunned from the impact, but her injuries were not life-threatening. Drakar thought he could remove the boulders, but even the slightest movement caused Kylan pain.

"Can you transform?" Drakar asked.

"Yes," Kylan said, "but I'm afraid these boulders will crush me in my smaller form."

"I am too tired to make her ephemeral," Skye said. "I don't have enough power left. But these rocks here," she said, pointing to the ones that pinned Kylan's wings, "they are not leaning against anything but Kylan, so nothing will collapse if I remove them."

"She will still be pinned," Drakar said.

"If you can support those boulders there, she can change to human form," Skye said, "and I can pull her free before the rest collapse."

Drakar analyzed the pile. The Tavinter's logic was sound. It would require speed and good timing, but it could be done.

"Does that sound reasonable?" he said to Kylan.

"It does. Let's do it."

And so Drakar propped up a good many of the larger boulders, Skye used the remainder of her strength to make a few of the smaller rocks disappear, and Kylan transformed, pulling herself from the pile before the entire thing collapsed. She rose to her feet, brushing the dust from her blue armor.

Skye collapsed, utterly exhausted, and Drakar caught her before she fell to the ground. He slung her about his torso as if she weighed nothing, carrying her easily on his back and supporting her legs with his arms. She had only to lean against him and he had her whole weight.

"So will someone explain what in the world happened here?" Drakar asked. He offered his arm to Kylan as they started down the long hallway, and he carried the Tavinter on his back.

"Skye was able to get us right in front of Volva, undetected," Kylan said. "But I had to materialize to affect her. I surprised her and easily got the upper hand, but then she led me into a trap. I would have been crushed, but Skye cast her spell on a dragon-sized block of stone that was about to fall on me, and made it disappear."

"That was hard," Skye said, her voice muffled as her face was buried in Drakar's back.

"I can imagine," Kylan said. "Then the last I saw was that Skye had reappeared and was fleeing for her life down this corridor." Kylan's voice trailed off as her gait slowed. She came to a stop. "Is that what I think it is?"

Drakar grinned. "Yes, yes it is."

Volva's long, golden tail was lying in the center of the hallway, blocking most of the entrance. Although enormous, it was a pathetic-looking thing, shriveled on one end and bloody on the other.

"That was actually easier," Skye mumbled into the back of Drakar's shirt.

"By the gods," Kylan murmured.

Skye leaned back far enough to have an articulate conversation. "I tried to kill her, but she was right on top of me, so I only got her tail. She could hardly fly without it."

"She will hardly be able to do anything without it," Kylan said, her own backside cringing in involuntary commiseration. "You may not have killed her, but you have accomplished our goal. Volva will be incapacitated for years, and can no longer interfere. It may take decades for that to grow back."

"If it grows back at all," Drakar said with satisfaction.

Kylan turned to the youngster who had once again buried her head in Drakar's back, and who was now almost asleep. The girl was astonishing, not only in her power but in her creativity in using it. Idonea had often commented that this creativity was what made mages potent, even when all else was equal.

"I don't think you should fly with those injuries," Drakar said, examining Kylan.

"Do you have something else in mind?" Kylan asked, a saucy tilt to her chin.

Drakar made an elaborate bow. "I would be happy to transport you, my lady." He handed Skye off to Kylan, then disappeared in a flash of red light. Kylan helped the Tavinter up onto his back, then climbed up herself. It was a novel experience, feeling Drakar's great muscles flex beneath her as he leaped skyward, for she had never ridden another dragon in her human form.

As she settled into his comfortable rhythm, leaning against one bony plate while the Tavinter slept in her arms, she thought perhaps she should do this more often.

Chapter 31

The row of saplings bordered the entire garden. There was no doubt in Raine's mind that these were cuttings from the Tree of Death, and that her actions had now spawned an Arbor of Death. True, it would take decades, possibly centuries for them to obtain the size of the tree she had destroyed, but when they were full-grown, their potential would be hideous.

Feray watched the Arlanian closely as the woman stared down at the twisted little seedlings, knowing that her vigilance was probably unnecessary. The Goddess had warned the mortal against further disobedience, threatening not her but her helpless, entombed lover. It had been enough to keep the Arlanian in check, to keep her from harming herself or anything else. Still, Feray watched as the mortal ran her fingers over the blue and gold markings on her forearms, unconsciously tracing their outlines. She had done this often of late.

"Do those hurt?"

"What?" Raine said. "No, they are scars, long ago healed. They are sensitive at times, but they don't hurt."

"I am surprised that Scinterians, being such fierce warriors, would allow anyone to do that to them, even another Scinterian."

Raine smiled a mocking smile. "Well, that's just it. I didn't 'allow' anyone to do anything to me."

Feray's expression communicated that she did not understand, so Raine continued.

"The hardest part of obtaining Scinterian markings is that they must be self-inflicted. It requires assistance, to a degree. But the act itself is always self-initiated. Believe me, it is harder to do this to yourself than to be held down and have someone else do it."

Raine's eyes were so pale a blue they seemed to glow like the fluorescent plants surrounding her.

"All of my worst wounds, past, present, and future, are self-inflicted. But always with a purpose."

The enigmatic words made Feray uneasy. She motioned that the mortal should return to Hel's chambers, and as she followed her, she determined to repeat the exchange to the Goddess later.

Hel gave one last, great thrust and then collapsed on her lover. She could feel the mortal's heart beating with the exertion of her climax, could feel the rise and fall of her chest as the Arlanian sought to catch her breath. This had been a particularly enjoyable session, for she had once again brought out the "blessed phallus" and demanded that her captive lover maintain eye contact with her the entire time she drove her to orgasm. Or at least until those beautiful purple eyes fluttered closed, unable to remain open as the body was wracked with spasms of pleasure.

Hel was content to simply lie there for an extended period of time, enjoying the coolness of the skin beneath her. Finally, she rolled over onto her side, her breasts pressed against the muscular arm as she toyed with the outlines of the ridged abdominals.

"Do you know the moment I love beyond all others?"

Raine had no desire to engage in pillow-talk with the Goddess, but she knew better than to ignore her. Still, she could not control her sarcasm.

"When I am 'writhing' beneath you, as you so poetically put it before?"

The sarcasm only amused Hel.

"No, I do love that. But there is a moment right before that," she said, tracing the curvature of the ribs, "a moment just before your eyes turn violet. The moment where, despite your every effort, you realize that you're going to give into me."

There was something dangerous in Hel's words, and Raine stiffened. The taunting was not unusual, but the trajectory of the conversation seemed to be veering into an unknown treachery.

Hel continued, her words spoken without malice, but utterly cruel. "It is the instant right before your body betrays you, that instant where all the strength of your father gives way to the weakness of your mother."

Raine sought to control her anger. She did not want to engage with the Goddess, but she could not help herself. "My mother was not weak," she said through clenched teeth.

"No," Hel said, then with a significant pause, "she was not."

It took a moment for the words to sink it, but in that instant, all of Raine's fears were confirmed. She began struggling wildly striking out at the Goddess with all her might. But Hel merely laughed at her, restraining her with her weight and her will. Still, the restraint was not accomplished easily, a fact that only seemed to please Hel.

"You are peculiarly strong," the Goddess said, "which makes your surrender all the more enjoyable."

The struggle went far longer than usual, with the Arlanian thrashing and fighting, but eventually Hel was able to subdue her with kisses, then by thrusting her breast in her mouth, triumphantly feeling not the bite she was prepared for, but a suckling filled with desperation. And she truly gained the upper hand when she was able to work the phallus back inside the Arlanian, pinning her to the bed with both her weight and the penetration. And the mortal moaned in both anguish and desire as Hel gently began working Sjöfn's infernal device, quickly giving Hel the moment she loved beyond all else, then everything else beyond it.

Chapter 32

kye slept for almost two full days on returning to the Ha'kan capital. She was rarely alone, for Dallan, Rika, Kara, and the Priestesses kept a constant rotation of curling about her in her bed. And Lifa, who had taken to napping as her pregnancy progressed, was happy to take her rest pressed against her beloved Tavinter. So when Skye awoke, it was to find the loveliness of the future High Priestess lying next to her.

"You had us all worried," Lifa said softly.

"Worried?" Skye said, her mind still muddled with sleep. "I'm fine. I was just tired."

"Kylan told us what you did, saving her and nearly killing Volva on your own."

"It was hardly on my own," Skye said, rubbing her bleary eyes. "I thought Kylan had her beat, but then Volva sprang a trap on her. I was running for my life and just got lucky."

Lifa kissed her forehead. The modesty and diffidence of her little Tavinter were as enduring today as they had been the first day she had seen her, seated on a bench at the Sjöfn Academy outside the Queen's throne room. Idonea had warned of the arrogance associated with magical power, but not a one of the Ha'kan thought that would be an issue with Skye.

"You can downplay it all you want. But when an Ancient Dragon sings your praises, you have accomplished something. But are you sure you're all right?"

Skye wrinkled her brow, for Lifa was persistent in her concern.

"I was just really tired, but I'm fine now." The feel of Lifa's breasts pressed against her arm finally registered on Skye, and her eyes drifted to them. "In fact..."

"Oh no," Lifa said, laughing. "I am under strict orders to send you to Y'arren as soon as you are up and about."

"All right," Skye said, her disappointment obvious.

"But," Lifa said, "the rest of my day is free. So once you are finished?"

Skye sprang out of the bed, invigorated. "I will be right back," she said, pulling on her clothes as she scrambled out the door, followed by the beautiful melody of Lifa's laughter.

Y'arren raised her head as the young Tavinter approached. The girl looked well, perhaps a bit pale, but there was a spring in her step. Idonea was seated next to her in the circle of stone benches, and as Skye neared, the wizened elf motioned for her to take the seat opposite her. Idonea, too, examined Skye closely.

Skye flushed under the scrutiny. "I'm fine, I assure you."

Y'arren smiled gently. "I'm sure you are, young one."

"Kylan told us what you did," Idonea said, "and we just wanted to make sure you're all right."

"Why wouldn't I be all right?"

Y'arren and Idonea exchanged significant glances, and Skye grew wary.

"What?"

"First tell me how you felt on this quest," Y'arren said.

"I felt fine," Skye said again, realizing that she was just repeating herself and the description was insufficient. She thought back.

"When I first cast the ephemeral spell on all of us, it was not hard. When I released Drakar from the spell, it grew easier. I began to grow a little tired as Kylan and I made our way through the castle, but I was able to release Kylan from the spell as well, when we came upon Volva. Then I had only to keep myself hidden."

"Until the stone fell."

"Yes," Skye said, then fell silent as she grew thoughtful. Y'arren and

Idonea exchanged another glance.

"I really didn't think I would be able to stop that stone," Skye murmured, half to herself, "I caught it right before it struck Kylan and made it pass through both her and the ground."

Skye toyed with a flower, caressing the silky petals with her fingers.

"And you reappeared to save Kylan?" Y'arren prompted.

"Yes," Skye said, fingering the plant. "I couldn't maintain the spell on myself and the stone at the same time. Then I had to run away, because Volva could see me."

"And yet you were able to cast the spell a final time, on an enormous object, while exhausted, and fleeing for your life."

"Yes, and—," Skye stopped, unable to put her feelings into words. Y'arren and Idonea waited patiently for her to gather her thoughts.

"And strangely, that was the easiest of all."

Y'arren rubbed the head of her gnarled wooden staff, an area worn smooth by this action over years. She sighed. It was as she expected.

"What?" Skye asked. "You act as if that was a bad thing."

"No," the ancient elf said, "not a bad thing. It can be a very good thing, but one not without consequences."

Skye turned to Idonea, who might better explain Y'arren's sometimes oblique pronouncements.

"I once told you what Isleif thought about pure light magic, that it was possible it could reach a tipping point and become self-sustainable, replicating almost without end. You may be nearing that tipping point."

"Me?" Skye said in disbelief. "I am hardly capable of that."

"That remains to be seen," Y'arren said. "And if it comes to that, you may be able to accomplish extraordinary things. Unheard of things. But it will come with a price."

"Yes," Skye said, "I remember the whole 'destroying the world' thing."

"That is one danger," Y'arren agreed, "but I'm beginning to think you can avoid that if you're not casting a destructive spell. But there will still be a price."

"What price?"

Y'arren rubbed the wooden head of her staff once more, staring down at its knotted surface.

"What price?" Skye said, turning to Idonea.

"There is the very real possibility your power will be exhausted," Idonea said. "You might never be able to practice magic again."

Skye did not have to long consider this option. "I don't care. I spent most of my life without magic. And if I can save Raine, then I will gladly give it up."

Y'arren nodded. "That is what I thought, but I could not allow you to proceed without knowing the risks."

Skye was adamant. "Raine has saved my life more times than I can count. And one time when I was standing right up there on that terrace," she said, pointing up to the passageway overhead, "when I felt lost because I was endangering everyone around me. She told me that one day I would save her. And I will take her words over any stupid prophecy."

Y'arren glanced up at the terrace. More she would have to meditate upon, another revelation from Raine. It seemed her goddaughter had left clues, particularly with this Tavinter. And those clues made it appear as if Raine was in a war of words with the gods themselves.

Chapter 33

Hel found Raine in the shrine, her back pressed up against the words of the prophecy, staring up at the empty eyes of her lover. The mortal had avoided this room for some time, for Hel had grown angry at the amount of time she spent sitting before Talan and had trapped her on the bench. She had dropped the Arlanian's pants around her ankles and gone down on her for an extended period of time, her hungry mouth and tongue driving the woman to orgasm, then climaxing herself as the mortal twisted about beneath her dragon lover's unseeing eyes. Hel would not have her possession pay attention to another, and she particularly enjoyed the captive audience, unseeing or not, of one who had spurned her.

Hel settled on the bench across from Raine, and regarded her Consort. The mortal had changed of late, perhaps yielding to her unending attentions with a degree of resignation. Her fate would not change. There were many things Hel wanted to try as she carried the Arlanian deeper and deeper into the world of sexual darkness that awaited her. Truly, she had been gentle thus far, but the mortal had proven remarkably resilient, a characteristic that would prove unfortunate for her future. Hel had no desire to harm her, but the thought that the Arlanian would both climax and survive, no matter what she did to her, thrilled and fired her imagination.

As much as Hel enjoyed physically tormenting the Arlanian, the mental games she played with her entertained her even more. She was ever-vigilant against any softening towards her, wary of any weakness or tender feelings that might arise, and perhaps the expression of that vigilance was her brutality.

"So," Hel said, "you seem to grow resigned to your position."

Raine's eyes drifted downward and settled on the Goddess, but she did not speak.

"I could see your many schemes and plans when I first brought you here. Your thoughts of escape. Even when I revealed the prophecy to you, I could see you still had hope. But at last, I see that hope is dying."

Raine still did not speak, merely sat staring mutely.

"Did you think to make me fall in love with you?" Hel said mockingly. "Did you think I would regret my actions? See the error of my ways? Did you think that I would grow soft and one day set you free?"

Raine could have denied any and every part of the conversation. But instead, she responded quietly, with a confidence that was devastating.

"I know that you will not fall in love me," she said, and then paused.

"Because you're still in love with Talan."

Hel did not flinch at the pronouncement, but it was a testament to the blow that she did nothing at all. She just sat there staring. Raine expected any response: laughter, denial, the infliction of violence, pain, even death. But instead, the Goddess just sat there, stunned by the perfect strike.

The two adversaries sat across from one another, one composed in her helplessness, one flustered in her omnipotence. At last, after what felt an eternity, the Goddess stood, smoothed her robes, and walked away.

Chapter 34

The dust of the Empty Land drifted to and fro on the horizon. The barren landscape looked even more forbidding than it had twenty-some years before. Idonea sat on her black stallion, wearing a long, maroon robe emblazoned with glyphs representing the interplay between dark magic and dragons. The vestments swirled about her in the gusts of wind as she held her staff at her side.

Feyden sat next to her on a white horse, eschewing the hardened armor of the high elves and instead wearing his personal armor, a greenish leather that moved as one with him. The elven markings on his jerkin told the history of his people. His sword glinted in the sunlight, its gold hilt polished to a high sheen, and his bow was strapped to his back.

Next to him, Lorifal was astride a brown horse, his stout figure solid in the saddle, his great axe slung over his shoulder. His horse was stockier than the others, shorter in the leg and more muscular, a perfect beast to accommodate the heavy burden of its rider in full dwarven armor.

To Idonea's right was Elyara of the Halvor, also dressed in the flowing garments of a mage, hers green where Idonea's were maroon, and covered with the yellow glyphs of the wood elves and the natural world. She, too, was astride a horse and bore a staff, one holding an orb illuminated with a soft green glow.

And at Elyara's side was her love of two decades, the one she had met on this same journey years ago. Dagna, Official Bard of the Empire, who bore a sword and a shield, the latter emblazoned with the crest of the current Empress. She wore light armor and rode a sturdy steed, for their journey would be long, this she knew.

Bristol also knew the length of the journey, and he had been a much younger man when they had made it before. But still he wore the heavy armor of a Knight Commander, his broadsword strapped to his back, his helmet tied to his saddle until it would be needed. It was likely days before they would meet an enemy or battle, but he was prepared nonetheless.

Skye was slightly behind the six, sitting on a blue roan that grazed placidly while she unconsciously stroked its neck. She wore the Tavinter leather armor with an eagle on her chest, the uniform of the First Ranger of the Ha'kan. Her sword hung at her side, her bow strapped to her back. There was a peculiar tension about her, as if she were balancing on some unsteady, unseen object, but displaying a confidence and certainty that Idonea had rarely seen in her.

"How are you feeling?" Idonea asked. "Are you certain you can do this? It's a very long journey."

If Skye had shown the slightest bit of indecision or doubt, they would go with a secondary plan. But Skye answered breezily.

"I feel good. I feel strong."

Idonea looked to her companions, the five who had made this journey with her so many years ago, when she had foolishly sought to steal the soul of an Ancient Dragon, and Raine had saved her. Raine had saved them all, time and again, and now it was time for them to repay her.

"Then cast your spell."

Skye did so, and the band turned translucent while the land around them remained solid.

Idonea nudged her steed, and it began trotting out across the forbidding desert, followed by the fluid-like horses of her companions.

Chapter 35

The Gardener was tending the saplings, and Raine lay on the bench on her back watching him. His transparent form bent over the small trees, preening them, talking to them, and generally just muttering to himself. He was quite mad, that was apparent, but Raine could not hear the nonsense that streamed from him. She could only see the contortions of his translucent face, but that was enough to give clue to his insane ramblings. She could not interact with him in his parallel world, and she wondered how he was able to interact with the plants, musing that it might have been the nature of the plants themselves. They were all unholy renditions of real plants, night jasmine, red flare, fluorescent gladiolas, similar enough to be recognizable, but with something dark running through their veins. Perhaps death itself ran through the stems, just like it ran in the golden sap of the young trees.

Usually the sight of the Gardener would fill Raine with dread, for it would bring forth the Goddess. Hel would enter the realm of the dead to speak with him, and his animated gesturing increased proportionally, making him appear even more unbalanced than his normal state. When she returned, she would invariably set her sights on Raine, and Raine would soon be on her back, on her knees, or pinned or tied in whatever position pleased Hel.

But Hel was gone right now, that much of which Raine was certain. As composed as she had been in her deadly verbal salvo, Raine knew there would be repercussions, and the way that Hel looked at her after that, with a seething intensity and a promise of retribution, made her body and blood turn cold. The assertion regarding Talan had been an educated guess, but it had landed with devastating effect.

But the Goddess of the Underworld wasn't in the Underworld, for Raine could breathe easier, did not feel as cold, and did not have the constant wariness that burdened her like a heavy cloak, its weight essential but exhausting. Feray and Faen took turns watching her, one or the other, if not both, never very far. But their attention did not weigh on her the way that Hel's did. Feray tended to blend into the background with circumspect efficiency, treating Raine much as she treated the Goddess. And Faen had given up taunting the mortal, rather simply watched her with his glowing eyes as his emotions regarding the Arlanian had grown so complex it hurt his head to think of her. Hatred, jealousy, fear, and grudging respect warred within him. One somehow overwhelmed the other three, although he still watched her, hopeful to see her commit some infraction he could gleefully carry back to his Mistress. The handmaidens were always a possibility, for they fluttered about her in a constant state of attempted seduction, but the mortal was steadfast in ignoring them. So he sat in his silent contemplation, engaging in more self-reflection than he had at any time in his long life.

Raine relaxed, staring up at the night sky which still held the constellations of Arianthem. She had feared that Hel would take them from her, and she probably would when she returned, but for now she would enjoy this one connection with home.

Chapter 36

Idonea gazed downward into the endless depths at the Edge of the World. They had moved slowly across the Empty Land, but unlike before, they had not had to battle an army of Hyr'rok'kin. In fact, they had met little life of any kind other than a few snakes and beetles. The Empty Land had been utterly desolate, and the band had only the elements to fight, a battle for which they were well-prepared.

Skye stood staring down into the emptiness below her and remembered Raine describing the vertigo that took hold at that place. It was difficult to tell if she was on a cliff looking down or on the ground looking into a massive hole, and the sensations alternated, causing dizziness and mental discomfort. Still, a shiver of excitement passed down her back. She was standing at a place very few in all of history had seen.

"How are you doing?" Elyara asked. Skye liked the kind, gentle elf, as well as her ribald companion, the imperial bard. They made an interesting couple, really quite opposite in all things. But one characteristic they shared became apparent the minute they set out on the quest: both were fierce, experienced warriors in their own way.

"I'm fine," Skye said, smiling. "This is really no strain at all."

"Good," Idonea said, "because I think from here on out, we should remain invisible."

The band had been invisible for the majority of the journey, uncloaking briefly to communicate, which was much easier in a solid state. The fact that Skye was able to maintain the spell even when she slept was a revelation to Idonea and did indeed support Isleif's supposition that Skye's magic could become self-sustaining. Idonea just hoped that it did not become like the ball of light: an unstoppable force gently bobbing along in a straight-line path, annihilating everything in its way.

"Not ephemeral?" Skye asked.

"No," Idonea replied. "Not yet. I don't want to overtask you. It's a long, steep trip down, and although I have no doubt of your physical conditioning, we need you to stay strong. We will have to leave the horses here."

At that pronouncement, the black stallion and blue roan transformed into Drakar and Kylan in their human form.

"Ah, that was enjoyable," Drakar said, who had carried his sister across the Empty Land.

"Hmm," Kylan said, less than convinced, "I think that's the longest I've been ridden without a climax at the end of it. You owe me, little Tavinter."

Skye turned bright red, wishing she could come up with any clever response. That was a debt she would gladly pay.

"Don't rattle her," Idonea said, "we don't want her to lose control."

"Not here, anyway," Kylan said, the double-meaning clear. Idonea cast her a scolding glance.

"Skye, go ahead and return us to invisibility."

Skye complied, and the band turned translucent to one another, and invisible to the rest of the world.

"One advantage of invisible over ephemeral is that we can see the landscape better," Skye said, remembering the disorientation of watching a transparent Drakar against the background of a transparent courtyard.

"We'll just have to watch our step," Idonea agreed.

The small band started down the trail leading into the Veil. "Trail" was a misnomer, for it was more like a highway now. Years before, preparations were being made to widen the path, but it had still been fairly narrow. Now it was broad with little danger of falling over the edge, built to accommodate the army of Hyr'rok'kin that had marched forth from it. Although the road was steep, it was smooth and the trek was not as difficult as decades before.

"Isn't it strange," Dagna said, "to see Idonea be the responsible one?"

"Indeed," Feyden responded as Lorifal chuckled, and Elyara muffled laughter with her hand.

"You may be invisible," Idonea said, "but I can still hear you."

Raine sat before Talan in the shrine. As usual, the sight of her lover brought her comfort. She had spent hours running her hands over the amber surface of the tomb, searching for any weakness or defect, always out of sight of the Goddess or her minions. She had even pounded upon it with her bare fists, then any implement she could find. But nothing had worked or had any effect. The surface was flawless.

So Raine sat before the silver-haired woman in the dragonscale armor, admiring her high cheekbones, her full lips, the golden eyes that stared out at nothing. She had no fear that the Goddess would catch her; Hel was still gone. Although Feray would probably report her vigil upon her return, that would be the least of the transgressions for which Raine faced punishment. And Raine thought that punishment would be great, for the Goddess had been gone longer this time than she ever had before.

The translucent figures came upon the thick vegetation that bordered the Veil. The trek down the Edge of the World was as uneventful as the crossing of the Empty Land. It required repeated periods of rest, even hours of sleep, but this time, there were no bands of Hyr'rok'kin roaming about. There weren't even any sentries. Fenrir had told Idonea that might be the case, for Hel's arrogance also tended to be her undoing. It was unfathomable to the Goddess that any would disobey her edict and risk her wrath. So they had reached the Veil without incident.

But a new danger inhabited this strange world. The forest was dense and would slow their progress. Acid lurked in the water. And although there were no Hyr'rok'kin, many creatures lived within the Veil, creatures that could sense magical energy. The shriek of Reaper Shards could be heard off in the distance, the high/low tone unmistakable, causing Skye to start. She had to still the beating of her heart, for the monstrosities terrified her. By the looks on the faces of those around her, she was not the only one who feared the abominations.

"How do you feel?" Idonea asked Skye for the hundredth time.

"This is actually getting easier," Skye said. "I feel like I'm hardly expending any effort. It's almost like the magic is doing it on its own."

That was both promising and worrisome to Idonea. She could feel the low thrumming of the power surrounding the girl, and it was indeed stable. Skye seemed to be reaching that tipping point that Isleif had described, which was a very good thing considering what she was about to do next.

"Can you make us ephemeral?" Idonea asked. "All of us?"

Skye considered the request. It should have been impossible, for the ephemeral spell was exponentially more difficult than the invisibility spell. But for whatever reason, the spell seemed not only possible, but almost inevitable.

"I can," Skye said with growing certainty, "without a doubt." She looked around, chewing her lip.

"What is it?"

"Well," Skye began. "I'm not sure how I know this, but there is one problem."

"What's that?" Elyara said, stepping forward. Y'arren had briefed her explicitly on the benefits and dangers of Skye's unique abilities.

"I can make everyone ephemeral," Skye said, "and the spell will sustain itself until I remove it. But once I remove it..."

"You're done," Idonea said, reading the girl's expression.

"Yes," Skye said, unsure how that made her feel. She reminded herself that the sacrifice was for Raine, and any reluctance due to self-interest evaporated. But she was reluctant for other reasons as well. "Once I remove the spell, I will not be able to cast it again."

Idonea sighed. That meant if they couldn't sneak Raine out, they would have to materialize to fight, and they would be unable to hide themselves to escape.

"So it might be a one-way trip," Feyden said, planting his translucent sword in the ground. "But I think we all knew that coming in."

"Aye," Lorifal said, "that we did."

"We'll fight," Dagna said. "We'll not leave Raine there."

"And we'll find your mother," Elyara said, putting her hand on Idonea's shoulder.

Bristol considered this new development. This had been a massive undertaking. They had prepared for every contingency, but had hoped to use none of them, thinking the Tavinter could get them in and out unseen and undetected. He admitted he had known in his heart that would not be the case. Dealing with Hyr'rok'kin was one thing; dealing with gods and demons another. He ran his fingers through his red hair.

"Well, if that's the way it's going to be, that's the way it's going to be."

Idonea turned back to Skye. "Then cast the spell, and we can walk right through the Veil."

The garden was dark, quiet, and peaceful, and Raine sat on the bench among the fluorescent flowers as a giant, glowing bee hovered near her. The bee was almost the size of a closed fist, but it was benign in its flight, interested only in the glowing pollen it harvested. It ignored the figure who watched it for a few moments, then drifted off in thought once more.

Surely her reprieve would not last much longer and Hel would return. She tried to enjoy what remained of her freedom, but it was difficult with the unknown sentence she faced. And although the length of time Hel was gone was a blessing, it was also unnerving, signifying that Hel's wounds were deep and that Raine would surely pay for their infliction. Time was hard to judge in the Underworld. Even the subtle changes of dim light barely differentiated the night from the day. How long had Hel been gone? A week? Longer? And where was she?

Fenrir had once spoken of Ásgarðr to her. He spent very little time in that realm, by choice, and she had the impression he was not favored there. Conversely, and surprisingly, both his father and his sister were the Allfather's favorites, and Fenrir speculated that this attention spoiled Hel as a child and contributed to her sinister development. Raine wondered if that was where Hel was now, somehow having worked her way back into her grandfather's good graces. If so, that was probably where she went to lick her wounds, dreaming up ways to make Raine suffer.

Raine sighed and started to stand up, then stopped. She slowly sat back down, a strange look on her face. Her actions caught the attention of Feray, who watched her closely, and of Faen, who examined her expression at length. But the mortal did not move, simply sat there, staring at the offshoots of the Tree of Death, deep in thought.

Raine struggled to keep an impassive expression on her face. She spent most of her time in a dark, pensive mood, so that was the disposition she attempted to portray. But she had just felt something, something she had not felt in a very long time, something that was far closer than it should be, something that was like a ray of light piercing through the darkness of the Underworld.

She felt Skye.

The Veil was considerably easier to walk through in an ephemeral state, Idonea thought. And they did not have to worry about whether or not it was thin enough for flesh and blood to pass through. Before, they had spent days hacking their way through the thick vegetation, avoiding poisonous plants and vines that bled acid. Gigantic slugs, toads, ambulatory mushrooms, all had been perils they faced before. They had been attacked by Reaper Shards and even the Membrane itself.

But this time, they were able to walk unimpeded through the translucent world around them. It was truly the most monumental spell that Idonea had ever seen, and she was saddened to think she might never see it again. And she was daunted by the fact that she was going to have to try and match it to hold one of the most powerful gods in all the realms.

The forest thinned, then cleared as two enormous gates rose up from the ground. Even in their transparent state, Hel's visage could be seen upon them, just below the inscription "where hope dies." And although all knew that they and their companions were invisible and untouchable, many shivered as they walked through the fluid-like barrier. Feyden wondered how they were going to get back out if Skye could no longer cast the spell, for they did not open the outer gates, but merely moved through them.

"This is the black and red courtyard," Feyden said to Skye. "It's kind of hard to see right now because everything is see-thru, but these tiles are all black and red, as far as the eye can see."

"I should like to see that in its normal state," Skye said, "but not enough to release the spell."

"I don't blame you," Feyden said, chuckling. "Let's stay like this as long as possible. The true Gates to the Underworld are at the far side of this courtyard, and it is a very long walk."

Raine napped, or at least pretended to nap, to calm the nervous energy that had taken over her being. She had not felt the presence again and desperately sought it, reaching out into the darkness. She was afraid that she had imagined it, a side-effect of the current tension threatening to overwhelm her. It would be a cruel hoax of her mind to suggest salvation when her damnation was so near.

When she opened her eyes, it was to find Feray watching her intently, even more so than usual. She was going to have to do something to dissuade that attention. Since she had few weapons at her disposal, she was going to have to use the one that was most reliable. She threw her legs over the edge of the bed, then pulled her shirt over her head.

Feray's eyes were magnetically drawn to the firm breasts and flat stomach. And when the Arlanian rose and dropped her pants to the floor, they went elsewhere with even less restraint. The mortal stretched, muscles bunched, flexed, then relaxed into gorgeous repose, then she padded across the floor barefoot and naked. She stepped down into the bath, the lovely, tight buttocks disappearing as she sat down waist-deep in the water.

"I want you to wash my back."

Feray started, for it seemed the mortal was talking to her. The mortal never asked anyone to bathe her. In fact, she disliked for the handmaidens to even touch her, and Hel often had them bathe her under her watchful gaze, enjoying the Arlanian's discomfort.

Raine looked over her shoulder, turning her violet eyes upon Hel's familiar. "Aren't you supposed to serve the Consort?"

This was tidy bit of reasoning and really all the encouragement Feray needed. She moved to the bath, removed her outer robe so that it would not get wet, then settled onto the ledge behind Raine. She lathered soap onto her hands, telling herself she would simply do the Arlanian's bidding then continue with her duties.

But she had vastly underestimated the allure of that doomed people. As soon as her hands touched that soft, silky skin, she was lost to the sensation. The scent of the woman was exquisite, and her head lowered so that she could press her lips against the shoulder. The taste was irresistible, and she did not want to break contact with that skin ever again. She found herself pressing against the back, her breasts pressing against the strong muscles, her hands working their way around to the front, her legs shifting forward to press her core against the strength of that torso…

Feray leaped up out of the bath, pushing away from the mortal as if she had burned her. Hel would destroy her for such an act, even in its unconsummated state. She snatched her robe from the ground and fled from the room.

Raine picked up the soap and began to lather her hands.

"Guess I'll just have to wash myself."

The two elves, the dwarf, the two imperials, the mage, the Tavinter, and the two dragons in human form stood before the true Gates of the Underworld. Six had stood here before, accompanied by another Ancient Dragon who had destroyed the Scales of Light and Dark, and a Scinterian who had slain the dragon who awaited them.

"So this is where we will leave you," Kylan said.

"Yes," Idonea said. "If all goes well, then perhaps we will be able to sneak out the way we came in."

Both Kylan and Drakar knew how unlikely that was going to be. Raine's greatest ability was now her greatest detriment. Her immunity to magic meant that Skye could not simply walk into the Underworld, make her ephemeral, and walk back out. They were going to have to figure out how to get her free, and that probably meant fighting. The fact that they didn't know where Talan was made it that much harder. The plan had been relatively simple up to this point. From here on out, it branched out into a thousand possibilities, some that were distinctly unpleasant.

"This gate was open before," Idonea said. "Ragnar used the Scales of

Light and Dark to pull it open in his attempt to bring back an age of darkness. Normally, only Hel has the power to open the gate, but Fenrir said that she needed Ragnar because she had lost the privilege."

Feyden thought back to the Hyr'rok'kin army that had staged in the Empty Land, a million strong. "Apparently she has regained that privilege."

"Yes."

It had been predetermined that Kylan and Drakar would wait in the red and black courtyard, a vast space that lent itself to their size and ability to fly. They were prepared for anything that came back through the Gates, including their fleeing companions, and whatever might be chasing them.

Drakar hugged his sister, and then Kylan did the same.

"You bring your mother back safe," the Ancient Dragon said.

Kylan and Drakar watched the band walk through the Gates in their ephemeral state when something occurred to Drakar. "If Hel is the only one who can open the Gates, what if they're not open when they return?"

"I think the plan relies on Hel's temper and her pride," Kylan said. "She threatened the mortal realm if her edict was disobeyed. I don't think she'll wait long to carry out that threat."

Raine moved back in the garden, now unencumbered by Feray's constant vigilance. Faen had disappeared as well, so only the demon guards on the terrace leading to the throne room were anywhere near. She sat on the bench as she so often did, looking at the saplings but no longer seeing them. Time passed, the light changed, but she did not move. Her senses strained the darkness around her desperately seeking the connection she craved.

Skye stood a few feet from her, struggling to control her emotions. Everything on the quest up to this moment had been exciting, exhausting, and exhilarating, a cacophony of experiences drowning out the grief and yearning she felt for her friend. But now, all she felt was the longing to reach out and touch Raine. She looked around her, careful that she was not occupying space with anything else, then transitioned from ephemeral to invisible.

Raine felt her instantly. She sat upright, still, unable to believe what she was sensing.

"Skye?" she whispered softly.

"I'm here," Skye whispered back.

The voice was at her right and Raine had to stop herself from reaching out and making her friend reappear instantly.

"We came for you," Skye continued, "I am here with the others. Idonea, Feyden, Elyara, they are all here."

This filled Raine with both joy and despair. She could not begin to hope that she might be freed.

"We just have to figure out how to get you through that throne room," Skye began. "The other door is blocked, but the passageway on the other side of the great hall is lightly guarded."

Raine's hope rose, but just as quickly was dashed. "There is a problem. Here, I must show you."

Raine stood up and glanced around the garden. She was still alone. She made her way to the stairs leading up to the bedchambers, then into the shrine room.

Skye let out a gasp. "Talan!"

"Yes," Raine said, pressing her hand against the amber prison. "Hel encased her in the resin from the Tree of Death. It is unbreakable. She has been comatose this entire time."

Skye looked up at the beautiful, silver-haired woman she had worshipped. The fiery red armor hugged her human form while gold eyes stared out lifelessly, a hand raised as if to ward off some unseen danger.

"Can you pull her from that prison?"

The idea excited Skye. "Yes, yes I think I can! But I'm going to have to fully materialize to do so."

Skye appeared and Raine was so happy to see her young friend she hugged her tightly. Skye clung to her as well, holding her perhaps even longer than the Scinterian held her. Skye turned her attention back to the amber prison.

"I should be able to make the amber ephemeral, and we can reach in and pull her out."

Raine readied herself to do so, and Skye laid her hands upon the smooth surface. She concentrated, but nothing happened.

"Hmm," Skye said, concerned, "that didn't do anything. My power might be waning."

Disappointment rose in Raine's throat like bile. "It might not be you," Raine said. "Idonea was able to destroy only a very small strand of it. Not even I have any effect against it. Its power is something other than magic."

"Then maybe I can make Talan ephemeral, and she will pass through the material."

"Try that!" Raine said, trying to moderate the enthusiasm that another failure would crush.

Again Skye raised her hands, concentrating, and again nothing happened.

"Damn!" she said, striking her fists on the unyielding surface.

Raine had to turn away, her disappointment so bitter it was choking her. She felt hot tears gathering in her eyes.

"Skye, I cannot leave her."

Skye was desperately trying to think. The prison was monolithic, too heavy for them to carry out or even dislodge from the stone wall. It seemed impossible that they would fail when they were so close to their goal.

"Maybe if we got you out," Skye said, hating herself for the suggestion and knowing Raine's response. "Maybe if you were free, we could regroup and come back again."

Raine's resignation was total. "I cannot leave her behind. Hel will kill her."

"Yes, I will."

Raine whirled around and snatched Skye to her, thrusting the girl behind her. Hel stood next to the amber prison, her expression as icy and volcanic as Raine had ever seen it. Her black robes flowed about her as Raine's breath came out as ice. The emerald eyes glowed and seethed with the fury of a god who had been affronted and defied. The green eyes flicked to the figure Raine held so protectively behind her.

"Ah," Hel said, smoothing her robes, "the one whom the sorceress would trade for you."

Raine's jaw clenched and Skye flinched. She had suspected as much of Ingrid.

"You're a pretty thing," Hel continued, "perhaps I will give you to my guards for their pleasure. Or better yet, I will add you to my collection," she said with a nod towards Talan's amber prison.

Raine slowly backed Skye from the room, keeping her behind her. She tried to think of anything with which she had to bargain. Hel had already been furious with her before; now her wrath was explosive.

"Your Majesty—"

"You will hold your tongue," Hel said coldly, "until I make use of it later." She turned back to Skye as she followed them.

"I must confess," the Goddess said, "traipsing into the Underworld is certainly daring. But you were a fool to come here alone."

Skye's response was as surly as it was bold.

"Who said I came here alone?"

And suddenly Skye was not alone, but surrounded by six heavily armed intruders. The demon guards were surprised by two imperials as Dagna and Bristol engaged them sword to pike in a ferocious attack. An elf and a dwarf menaced Hel with their bow and axe, but before Hel could laugh at their pitiful and ineffectual attack, Idonea raised her arms and cast an ancient and malevolent spell. Red glyphs carved themselves into the ebony stone of the ground and red light split out in all directions, forming a pyramidal cage which enclosed Hel.

"What is this?" she demanded, waving her hand as if to brush the spell aside.

But the cage did not move. The red light sparked, then stabilized, and Idonea grounded herself to maintain the spell.

"Ah, the dragon's daughter," Hel said sarcastically. "You, too, will pay for this indignity. And let me guess where you found this little spell."

Raine watched in amazement as the spell held against Hel's dreadful onslaught. She recognized the cage, and silently thanked Fenrir. It was apparent that Hel also knew where the cage had come from, and how it had been thwarted. She turned to Raine.

"You can end all of this right now by walking over here and touching this cage. I will let your friends go and we can pretend this never happened."

Raine wavered at this offer and Hel saw her opening. "I will even free Talan. Only you will remain here."

This stopped Raine in her tracks. If Hel would release her friends and her love, it would be worth it to know they were safe. She could endure anything to save Weynild.

"She's lying, Raine," Elyara said softly. "She is the daughter of the father of lies. She will kill us all."

Hel gnashed her teeth in fury, and Raine was persuaded by Elyara's quiet logic. She glanced to the growing tumult on the terrace of the throne room and knew that the alarm was being sounded. "You should go help Dagna and Bristol," she said, nodding to Feyden and Lorifal, and the two disappeared, sword and axe swinging, into the brawl outside. "Idonea, can you hold her?"

"I can," Idonea said, gritting her teeth.

"Then follow me," Raine said to Skye and Elyara, returning to the shrine room.

"You will not be able to hold me long," Hel said disdainfully, "even now I can feel you weakening."

"Shut up," Idonea said, infuriating Hel even more. There was no danger in making her mad, Idonea thought. If she was unable to hold Hel, she would be the first to die.

Elyara gasped when she saw Talan. The wood elves worshipped the dragons, and Talan'alaith'illaria above all others. It was painful to see the elegant woman so reduced, and even more painful to know the effect this must have had on Raine.

"Can you think of any way to get her out of here?" Raine pleaded.

Elyara thought furiously, and she and Skye exchanged hopeless glances. A new tumult of noise attracted Raine's attention and she ran back into the bedchambers.

"There," Idonea nodded at the main door, "there!"

It was Faen, having come in the other door from the hallway, the one that was always locked. He stared in dumb disbelief at the sight of his Mistress imprisoned in a cage of light, and a handful of mortals beating a demon guard squadron to death on the terrace.

"Faen," Hel hissed at him, "sound the alarm! And release the Hyr'rok'kin through the gates!"

Raine tried to catch him, but the spry demon was too fast and too close to the door. He was also driven by a fear of Raine, and an even greater fear of the Goddess, who was angrier than he had ever seen her. He sprinted back through the door from which he came, slamming it in Raine's face. It was once again as immovable as it had always been, no matter how hard she strained against it.

"Damn!" Raine said, then turned back into the room.

Hel watched Faen's departure with satisfaction. "Your window of opportunity is closing, Raine. Your mage grows weaker," she said, nodding to Idonea. "You can free me now and take my deal, or I will destroy everyone when I break free myself."

Raine again wavered and Idonea shook her head. "I've got this Raine."

But the strain on Idonea's face was evident, as was the indecision on Raine's. She leaned through the doorway into the shrine.

"Anything?"

Elyara looked crestfallen and Skye morose. They both shook their heads.

"I've never seen anything like this material," Elyara said. "It's not of the natural world. I don't know how to free Talan."

A crashing noise brought Raine back out of the room and she moved to the opening to the throne room. Faen had clearly done his duty, for there were demons rushing in everywhere from the hall below. The only thing keeping the four at the top from being completely overwhelmed was the staircase was a bottleneck of sorts. Raine grabbed a pike and cleared an entire swath of the monstrosities, but they were quickly replaced by others. And an endless stream was beginning to pour through the many doors into the throne room below.

"Raine."

Her name was spoken with a strained intensity, and she answered Idonea's summons.

"I don't know how much longer I can hold this."

Raine assessed the situation. Her comrades nearly overwhelmed on the stairs, her love still trapped in the amber prison, Faen off to release the Hyr'rok'kin into the mortal realm, and Hel on the verge of being loosed. She turned back to the Goddess, but this time Hel read her expression and just laughed.

"Oh no, my love, the deal is off the table. You had your chance, and you squandered it. Everyone here will die. Everyone except you, and you will wish for death." As if to punctuate her threat, the red light of the cage flickered as Idonea staggered, then stabilized as she regained her balance. Hel's eyes did not leave Raine as she smiled an evil smile. "I will fuck you on their corpses, and rape you on their graves."

"Well, isn't that a pleasant sentiment."

A portal flashed into existence and a beautiful woman with long white hair strolled through it into the room. Before Idonea had time to determine if Ingrid's presence was a good or bad thing, to guess whether the sorceress had come to help or to commit her final betrayal, Ingrid answered with her actions. She threw up her hands, added her dark power to the spell, and Hel was again fully contained. The Goddess fairly sputtered with rage.

"You! YOU!"

Ingrid cast an admiring glance at Idonea's heaving bosom. "You still owe me," her gaze flicked to Skye who stood in the doorway, looking at her with boundless gratitude. "And I would miss my monthly romp with my little Tavinter."

The Goddess had once terrified the sorceress, and in a way, still did. But when one was facing almost certain death, resignation tended to muffle fear. She ignored the fury of the being she was now helping to hold in check. "I don't suppose you have anything else up your sleeve?" Ingrid asked, "otherwise we're going to die, and that one's going to get raped on our graves," she said, nodding to Raine.

"Fortunately, Isleif and your little Tavinter had a Plan B," Idonea said, still wrestling to contain Hel.

Drakar and Kylan stood before the opened Gates of Hel, watching the Hyr'rok'kin army begin to pour forth into the red and black courtyard. They were still under the ephemeral spell, still in human form, arms crossed, watching the horde vomit from the Underworld.

"I guess that answers our question as to how we're going to get the gates opened," Drakar said.

"Yes," Kylan said, her sarcasm evident. "One problem solved."

"And I'm also guessing we should prepare ourselves to be released from this spell."

"Right again, my handsome boy."

The tumult on the terrace was unabated. There were screams of pain and fury, the clanging of metal on shield, the curses and roars of Lorifal, the exclamations of Bristol and Dagna. Skye and Elyara joined the battle on the staircase, the Tavinter adding her unmatched archery skill and Elyara her magic. Still, it was clear to Raine that Ingrid's arrival had merely delayed the inevitable, for Hel still strained against the cage, making headway against the power of the two mages.

The courtyard was now full. It seemed that every demon in the Underworld was in the great hall, drawn to the plight of their Mistress and in a blood lust to kill the intruders. Whoever struck down these interlopers surely would be rewarded beyond imagination. Skye was forced to switch to her sword when one large demon forced his way past Bristol and engaged her directly. She danced out of his way, using misdirection and speed to counteract his much greater brute strength.

"Ah, you are a nimble little thing. I will try to just wound you in hopes the Goddess will give you to me." He leaned back with a leer. "Maybe just cut off your legs at the knees, still leave all the good parts."

Skye shoved him back in disgust, but he pressed forward once more, his foul breath in her face. He used the throng around her to pin her against the wall, raising his bloody axe to carry out his threat.

"A handful of mortals," the demon sneered. "You should never have come to the Underworld alone."

"I'll say it again," Skye said between clenched teeth, "what makes you think I came alone?"

An explosion of light filled the throne room, and three swords materialized in the body of the demon, one held by the Dallan, the Princess of the Ha'kan, Rika, her future First General, and Torsten, Skye's second-in-command. The demon could not process this impossibility, and died before any of it sunk in. Dallan wrenched her sword from his body and turned it on the stunned adversaries surrounding her, as did her First General, her Ranger, and her friend.

Similarly, demons died throughout the great hall, impaled by the weapons that materialized as their warriors did. The throne room was filled with Alfar soldiers and Tavinter rangers, all fighting close quarters and using their element of surprise to devastating effect. The demons screamed and ran, trampling over one another in their panic, for they were trapped and surrounded by the army that had appeared.

The Hyr'rok'kin in the red and black courtyard were similarly surprised by the two enormous dragons that appeared right in front of them. And if that was not enough to sow terror, when the two dragons took flight, they revealed an army of imperials and Ha'kan behind them. On each flank, a regiment of dwarves appeared, the heavily armored soldiers letting loose their fierce battle cry.

Senta, First General of the Ha'kan, looked across the courtyard to Nerthus, Knight Commander of the Imperial Realm. They nodded grimly to one another, and Senta raised her sword.

"Charge!"

The din in the throne room had increased exponentially, and Raine looked askance to Idonea.

"Skye hid an army," Idonea said, shrugging. "Actually, two. We left one in the courtyard to stop the Hyr'rok'kin."

Despite their desperate situation, Raine had to grin. Leave it to Isleif and Skye to do the impossible. That old wizard had seen far into the future.

"But," Idonea said, the fatigue in her voice evident, "we have a problem."

Hel had stood quietly, utilizing every bit of her strength to fight against the barrier. She smiled an evil smile at this latest pronouncement.

"You're losing her," Raine said.

"We cannot contain her much longer."

And that would end everything, Raine thought. If Hel joined the fight, all would be lost. She could freeze mortals in their tracks, annihilate swaths of troops with a wave of her hand, bind her with those hideous dark tendrils while she watched everything she loved destroyed.

It is time.

The voice whispered in her head, the low, husky voice of one she loved. She closed her eyes as the silken tones caressed her ear, and she could feel the breath of her love on the nape of her neck. It was the voice of one who had seen further than anyone, an Ancient Dragon whose sight into the future was unmatched, a vision that Raine had held close and followed from the day they met.

It is time.

A dramatic change came over Raine. For the first time since Idonea had seen her in the Underworld, the warrior looked herself again. She stood up to her full height, her shoulders squared, the blue and gold markings rose on her skin, and her eyes were a flint-like blue. The only thing that frightened Idonea was the look of absolute resignation on her features. She walked from the room to find Skye.

An area had been cleared around the Tavinter, her friends having defended her then provided space for her to rest. Idonea's and Skye's contributions were equal, the difference being in intensity. Skye had maintained the invisible and ephemeral spells for days, releasing them only for brief periods, whereas Idonea was expending everything she had in a matter of minutes. It was hard to say which was more difficult: hiding an entire army, or restraining an angry god.

Dallan had kept a close eye on her beloved friend, and saw when Raine approached her. It was good to see the Scinterian warrior, but the look on her face concerned Dallan. And when Skye and Raine engaged in an intense conversation, with much distraught gesturing on Skye's part and calm insistence on Raine's, Dallan tried to move closer to overhear. It was evident that whatever Raine was telling Skye deeply distressed her, but she could only hear snippets of the conversation.

"You cannot ask me to do that!"

Raine put her hands on Skye's shoulders. "You must do this. When I give the signal, you cannot hesitate or all is lost. Trust me."

Skye was unhappy, that much was clear, and Raine walked stoically back to the doorway of Hel's bedchambers, casually killing two demons bare-handed on her way. She stood in the entrance, every once in a while glancing over her shoulder to judge the retention of the Goddess.

The dragons rained down fire and ice upon the hapless Hyr'rok'kin as the troops were trapped on three sides by the enemy, and to the rear by their own. The surprise attack had been enormously effective, and the bodies of the filthy beasts were strewn about and the red and black courtyard was now mostly red with spilled blood.

Still, the Hyr'rok'kin army greatly outnumbered their foes, and they continued to march through the gates in never-ending numbers. Although the Ha'kan, imperials, and dwarves had been chosen for their size and strength to hold the courtyard, they were slowly losing ground to the infinite horde. Senta assessed their situation grimly. They could fight the Hyr'rok'kin for hours, keep them from breaking or penetrating their ranks, but even so, they would eventually be pushed clear across the courtyard and trapped against the outer gates.

Finally, Idonea and Ingrid could hold the Goddess no more, and the red cage exploded outwards in a blinding flash of red light. Hel lifted both women with a wave of her hand and flung them across the room as if they were rag dolls. Raine raised her hand, giving the signal to Skye, but Raine's heart fell when she saw Skye hesitate.

Hel threw out her hand in fury, immobilizing Raine.

"I don't know what you think you're going to do," the Goddess said, "but you're not going anywhere."

She raised her hand again, and swept an entire cohort of elves from the terrace.

"But everyone else is going to die."

An enormous wolf sprang through the doorway past Raine, and leaped upon the Goddess. His great jaws closed upon her neck and his claws stabbed her through the midsection. She shrieked in fury and pain, a noise so horrible it caused all who heard it to tremble.

The paralysis fled, and Raine could again move. She had the momentary hope that Fenrir could defeat Hel, possibly even kill her, but that was quickly dashed. Hel flung the wolf god to the side much as she had flung Idonea and Ingrid across the room.

But his attack had done some damage, and Hel staggered, even went to one knee before she pulled upright once more. Raine saw Idonea stir.

"Idonea," Raine called out, "can you cast the spell again?"

Idonea was dizzy and disoriented, and she tried to understand what had happened. Something had struck Hel a terrible blow. Ingrid began to stir at her side.

"Perhaps together we can."

Hel assessed the situation and determined she was not going back in the cage. Even wounded, everything was in her favor and she spelled this out for Raine.

"If you leave," she said, her words dripping with venom. "I will kill Talan. And then I will come for you. And regardless, I will punish every single being who has been a part of this sacrilege."

And with that, the Goddess of the Underworld turned and entered the realm of the dead.

"No!" Idonea cried out, casting the spell, but too late. Hel's transparent form could be seen walking through the bedroom, then out the doorway exiting to the garden.

Raine sighed. Hel's words were true. She would never give up, and Raine had always known this would end in only one way. She looked fixedly at Skye.

Dallan saw the strange, brooding look from Raine, and turned to Skye. Very slowly, the Tavinter raised her bow and aimed straight at Raine. She had tears running from her eyes.

"No!" Dallan screamed, realizing what was about to happen.

Skye loosed the arrow, it flew true, and impaled Raine right through the heart. The arrow protruded from her torso as she looked down, fell to her knees, and then collapsed, dead.

"Skye!" Dallan screamed again. She ran over to her friend. "What are you doing? Why would you do that?"

Skye swallowed hard, tears still streaming down her face.

"Because she told me to."

Idonea and Ingrid both stared at the impossibility before them, and Fenrir buried his great head in his paws. Raine lay dead on the floor, the arrow sticking out of the chest that no longer rose and fell. Despite the noise of the battle outside the room, it was suddenly very, very quiet in the bed chamber.

Raine's body turned translucent. The ebony floor could be seen through her form. Then the spirit got to its feet, brushed herself off, then slowly walked across the room. She exited through the open double doors that led into the garden, following in the footsteps of the Goddess.

Hel wandered through the garden, fairly humming to herself. She cared little of what was happening outside; it was immaterial to the final result. Once in the realm of the dead, her pain had disappeared, and she was already savoring the revenge she would unleash once healed. She was startled by the presence of another.

The Goddess stared in disbelief and growing delight at what stood before her.

"What you have done?" Hel said. She stared at Raine, then at the arrow, unable to believe her good fortune. "You are now in my realm permanently. True," she said, half to herself, "you will eventually bend to my will and be entirely in my control, but that may take centuries. And even as my thrall, you will bring me pleasure." Hel was thoughtful. "As much as I have enjoyed your resistance, I weary of it and will revel in your subservience."

Raine did not appear that interested in this soliloquy. She plucked a flower from a stem, satisfying herself that the dead could indeed interact with the plants as she surmised. When she finally spoke, she changed the subject almost at random.

"My immunity to magic," she said casually, "has always been my greatest gift." She tossed the flower aside and plucked another. "One very common misconception, however, is that I deflect the spells that are cast my way."

Although the subject of conversation was extremely arbitrary, Hel was content to let the mortal ramble. Death often scrambled the brain.

Raine paused for a moment, absorbed in yet another flower. "Scinterians deflect magic," she continued absently. "Arlanians, on the other hand, Arlanians absorb it."

Raine turned around and gave Hel a very hard look.

"Guess whom I take after?"

Hel began to listen to what the mortal was saying. A danger was in there, lurking somewhere, but Raine was not going to wait for her to figure it out.

"Do you know what that means?" She plucked another flower and threw it aside. "For three hundred years, every spell that has been cast my way, every item that I have disenchanted, every seal that I have broken, every bit of that magic, is contained within my being."

The danger was beginning to coalesce, and what the Arlanian was describing was daunting, even to a god. Still, Hel was dismissive.

"You cannot use it," Hel said defiantly, "you are immune to it."

"I cannot use it," Raine agreed, pausing, "but the one that I am bound to can."

And from behind the mortal stepped Talan'alaith'illaria, Queen of all Dragons, her golden eyes glowing with molten fury. Her expression was so formidable Hel actually took a step back as Raine's words and their meaning sank in.

"You are bound to one another?"

"We are," Raine continued as Talan took another step towards the Goddess. "Which means that my soul could not leave the living realm without her. Which freed her from the prison you made for her by pulling her into this realm."

All of the implications converged on Hel at once, but Raine summarized them for her anyway.

"The Dragon's Lover," Raine began, "felled by the closest of allies." She looked with disdain at the arrow in her chest, pulled it from her torso, and threw it to the ground. "Carries into death without dying," she cast a significant glance at Talan, "that which saves all worlds."

Raine turned her gaze back to the Goddess, and there was no pity in her ice-blue eyes, only absolute judgment. "You see, I did know the translation of the final line of the prophecy. I have always known it. And it is my destiny to be the Consort of the Queen of the Underworld."

She paused before she delivered the final blow.

"That's just not going to be you."

With a roar, Talan struck the Goddess, channeling all of her rage, all of Raine's suffering, and three hundred years of magic, into an insurmountable weapon. The strike sent Hel to her knees, not only pummeling her but beginning to drain her as well. And as Hel's power diminished, Talan's power grew. The power exchange was reflected in Talan's appearance, for her garb changed, gradually transitioning into a stunning combination of Hel's robes and her own dragonscale armor. Her headdress was magnificent, Hel's crown intermixed with dragon horns. When the transfer of power was at last complete, Talan stood resplendent, the dragon as Goddess, while Hel was curled in a ball on the floor.

Raine looked at Talan approvingly. "Now that," she said with appreciation, "is a look."

Talan raised her own hand and with an imperious wave that put Hel to shame, changed Raine's garb as well. Now Raine was clothed in a perfect blend of her Scinterian armor and Arlanian clothing, the lovely purple garments providing the underclothing for the gleaming Scinterian leather.

"Now that," Talan said, "is what my Consort should wear."

And the dragon took her lover in her arms, kissing her with a passion that was unmatched in any realm. The kiss took Raine's breath away, caused her head to spin, and erased every ugly action that had been perpetrated on her with its pure love. Truly, the two could have stood there forever in one another's arms, were there not more pressing matters at hand. The silver-haired woman drew back from her young lover.

"Shall we go finish this?"

Raine grinned, loving the confidence, the regal elegance, everything about her soulmate.

"We shall."

Talan held out her hand and for once, Raine assumed the position of escort willingly and with pride. She walked at the side of the Goddess, her heart bursting in her chest.

The bed chamber was empty, for all within had moved to the terrace to continue the fight. The demon army had been pushed down the steps, so the terrace itself was nearly empty.

"Is that Talan?" Rika said, looking up in disbelief.

All those near her, Feyden, Dallan, Lorifal, all looked up at the mesmerizing sight of Talan. She was dressed as none had ever seen her, in a manner that was truly god-like. She glowed with a fiery, reddish-gold light, and her amber eyes looked out over her kingdom with disdain. Skye was ecstatic to see Raine at her side, who was also dressed in an extraordinarily beautiful manner. Both emanated an astonishing power.

Talan raised her hand, a scepter appeared, and with a single wave, she demolished the armies of the Underworld. Demons went up in flames and turned to ash, crumbling to the ground or winking out of existence. In the red and black courtyard, Hyr'rok'kin screamed in agony, turned to stone, and then crumbled into dust in one single motion. The mortal troops in the courtyard stood staring in confusion as the enormous army just disappeared into piles of rubble and dirt. As the echoes of the cries faded away, Senta prodded at a pile of the ash with the tip of her sword.

Drakar landed and transformed, followed by Kylan. They both glanced around at the soot and ashy remains, trying to grasp what had just happened. Drakar knelt down and rubbed some of the dust between his fingertips.

"Why," he asked, both sardonic and hopeful, "do I have the feeling this my mother's doing?"

Kylan just smiled.

A great cheer went up in the throne room of the Goddess of the Underworld. And the newly anointed Goddess took her Consort in her arms and kissed her, eliciting an even greater cheer from all present. The Alfar and Tavinter were joined by their excited brethren, the Ha'kan, imperials, and dwarves, who poured into the hall behind them. Many joyful reunions took place as Bristol hugged his fellow Knight Commander, Senta found her Princess and future First General, and Lorifal was pummeled by a throng of his fellow dwarves. Feyden was surrounded by his Alfar soldiers, who proudly stood at his side. Elyara and Dagna found one another, and Dagna lifted the slender elf off her feet in a bear hug. Kylan and Drakar entered the back of the room, and Drakar stared up in wonder at the terrace above.

"Is that my mother?"

Talan, unwilling to release Raine, gathered her daughter into their mutual embrace. Skye stood some distance away, next to Ingrid, then cast her a sideways glance.

"I knew you weren't completely evil."

"Not completely," Ingrid agreed.

The throne room of the Goddess of the Dead had never seen such revelry, and Fenrir stood in the shadows, the only one with concern on his features. It was not long until his concern was justified.

Lightning began to flash across the night sky above them, then a blinding bolt flashed downward accompanied by deafening thunder. Everyone stood blinking and covering their ears, many having crouched down to avoid the unknown.

The Allfather stood at the bottom of the stairs. His long beard and long gray hair flowed with the violence of his arrival, and the gold crown atop his head glinted with painful brightness to eyes already blinded by lightning. His handsome, craggy features expressed a myriad of emotions as his piercing blue eyes swept out over the assembly. He wore gleaming gold armor and auspiciously bore a scepter in his hand rather than the sword that hung at his side. No mortal present had ever seen him before, but all recognized him instantly. The assembly as one went to a knee, all save Talan and Raine, who remained standing as they guardedly assessed his arrival.

"What is this?" the Allfather said, his eyes again sweeping the crowd, his voice booming much like the thunder that had accompanied his entrance. His piercing gaze flicked to the bed chambers above, as if he could see right through the walls.

"A god has fallen? Mortals in the Underworld?"

His chastising gaze fell upon Fenrir. "God against god? Brother against sister?"

His gaze at last settled upon Raine and Talan. Surprisingly, any rebuke or admonition he held was not directed at them. In fact, his expression was one of slight admiration.

"Talan," he said. "One of my very favorite creations." He started up the steps toward her.

Talan watched his approach with equal parts wariness and respect. She was uncertain what his presence meant.

"Talan," the Allfather repeated. "Is it truly your wish to be the Goddess of the Underworld?"

Talan did not have to think long on this question.

"Of course not," the dragon said. "I did this to save Arianthem, and to save my love."

The Allfather nodded, as if this were evident to him. "Then I shall make you a deal."

Now Talan was even more wary as she awaited the Allfather's words.

"If you return the Underworld to Hel, I will guarantee that she will trouble the mortal realm no more. I will return you to Arianthem, as well as everyone here, safely, in the blink of an eye, to their homelands. And if you do this, I will give you your greatest heart's desire."

With this final phrase, the Allfather glanced to Raine, as did Talan.

"My greatest heart's desire?" Talan queried, as if testing the Allfather to see if he truly knew what she wanted.

"Yes," he said with supreme confidence. "Your greatest heart's desire."

Talan mulled the offer. She did not wish to be a god and did not wish to live in the Underworld. In fact, she did not wish to ever see it again. Raine stood quietly at her side while Talan considered the proposition. Raine was uncertain what exactly was being traded, but she herself had no desire to stay in the Underworld, although she would have consented to such a fate to stay with her love.

"Then I accept your offer."

Gasps accompanied the response and the Allfather was nearly jovial. "Then so be it."

With a wave of his hand, Talan's garments returned to her normal dragonscale armor, and she wore only a simple, elegant circlet on her head. Raine assessed the change with a critical eye.

"You're right, I like that much better."

Things were happening so quickly that it was hard for everyone to process the events. A heady joy, even elation was beginning to settle on the crowded room. They would all soon be home, safe and protected. This elation was dashed as Hel strode back onto the terrace, fully healed and fully clothed in her robes once more, her expression furious. She took a menacing step towards Talan and Raine, neither who budged.

"You will stop yourself now," the Allfather said sharply. His tone brooked no argument and was filled with disapproval. His granddaughter had displeased him, and in the unpredictable logic of the gods, he was more disappointed in her because she had been defeated than because of the wickedness of her actions. Had she been successfully evil, he might have been more inclined to overlook her deeds.

Perhaps it was this moral ambiguity that Hel appealed to in her next maneuver. "All may return to the mortal realm as you have decreed," Hel said bitingly, "but Raine is dead."

The implication in this caused Talan to put her arm about Raine as Hel continued.

"She may not belong here, but nor does she belong in the mortal realm. She must go to Valhöll, Vólkvangr, or even the Holy Mountain, but she cannot return to Arianthem."

Talan saw with a sinking heart that the cleverness of this argument appealed to the Allfather. "That is true," he mused.

A multiplicity of dangers hid in this suggestion, Talan knew. Raine occupied a strange space of being right now, and their bond might no longer keep them together. Not only might Raine be separated from her, but she could be sent to places where Hel could walk without restriction. She would not allow the Allfather to renege on their deal, and was furious at Hel's trickery and the Allfather's potential duplicity.

"I have already defeated one god today," Talan said in a low, dangerous tone.

The stunning threat took the Allfather aback, and he was again awash in the mercurial moods of the gods, uncertain whether to be proud of one of his greatest creations or to strike her dead on the spot. And although he wouldn't admit it, a very small part of him wondered if it was a legitimate threat.

"You would stand against me?" the Allfather asked, as if speaking to a recalcitrant child. "You are formidable Talan, but not even you can defeat the Allfather."

Hel smiled coldly, for she was already unraveling the victory that Talan had won, but a calm, soothing voice froze the smile on her face.

"She will not stand against you alone."

An extraordinarily beautiful woman stepped out of the shadows onto the terrace. She had alabaster skin, glowed with a soft golden light, and wore, long white robes that draped the graceful curves of her body. She had startling deep blue eyes, and for some strange reason, she looked familiar to Raine.

"You would stand against me in this matter, Sjöfn?"

"I would," the Goddess of Love said.

"Why?"

Sjöfn's eyes settled on Raine. "The Arlanians were the most cherished of all my children, and Raine the most cherished of all Arlanians."

The Allfather seemed entertained by this turn of events, but steadfast.

"Although your charms and wiles are formidable, Sjöfn, you are not known for your skill on the battlefield."

"I, however, am."

An ebony-skinned giant stepped from the shadows on the opposite side of the terrace. He was a perfect specimen of physicality, heavily armored, muscles bulging, a number of scars attesting to past battles. He was fiercely handsome, his dark eyes glowing with a dangerous light beneath his golden helm.

"Tyr," the Allfather said, "and you would stand against me as well?"

"I would," the God of War said. His fierce gaze settled on Raine. "The Scinterians were the most honored of all my children, and Raine the most honored of all Scinterians."

The Allfather considered this rebellion with far more equanimity than would be expected. It seemed that both Tyr and Sjöfn had made arguments more compelling than Hel's. At long last, he simply shrugged his shoulders.

"Only a fool battles love and war at the same time." He turned back to Talan. "Hel will return as Goddess of the Underworld. You will return to the mortal realm and receive your greatest heart's desire, and Raine," the Allfather at last turned to the one so favored by his pantheon, both to her benefit and detriment. "Raine, I will give you a very special gift. You may walk in all realms, the Underworld, the mortal realm, Valhöll, Völkvangr, the Holy Mountain, even Ásgarðr itself."

Raine bowed very formally in acceptance. "Thank you, Allfather. But I think I will return to the mortal realm."

And once again, the throne room erupted in cheers.

Chapter 37

Raine stirred from sleep, and her first thought was that she was warmer than she had been in quite some time. As her eyes opened, she realized that was because she was cocooned in soft hide blankets and furs in a giant nest, curled about her dragon lover. Weynild gazed down at her, content upon awakening to simply gaze upon the young woman at her side.

"We are home," Raine breathed out, her eyes as violet as the lavender in the fields.

"We are," Weynild said, brushing the fair hair from those eyes.

They were in Weynild's mountain keep, little more than a gigantic cave in a mountainside, but also Raine's favorite place in the world. This was where she had first come across the dragon decades before, falling in love with the creature upon first sight. It was where Weynild had taken the Arlanian Scinterian to bed, astonished that such a one had never bedded another, and where they had completed the Ceremony of Binding so that they could never truly be apart.

"Do you think the others made it home?" Raine asked.

"They probably woke up at home in bed, just like we did, wondering if the whole thing was a dream."

This thought comforted Raine. "How long have you been awake?"

"A few hours. I wanted you to rest." The golden eyes flicked upward to the cave opening and the fading light beyond, then to the lengthening shadows around them. "You're going to need it for what happens next."

The teasing tone brought Raine upright in the bed. "What happens next?"

"Hmm, you should probably go stand over there before the sun goes down."

"What?" Raine asked in bemusement, but Weynild only laughed and waved her hand. "Go over there."

Raine grinned and complied. Her love was positively playful right now, so Raine stood where Weynild directed her, the dragon content to lounge in bed and admire the naked form in the fading light.

"What is happening to me?"

"Hmm," Weynild said noncommittally

Raine looked down at her body. Having been entirely immune to magic her entire life, she had never experienced what she was feeling now. Her shape was shifting, her limbs transforming, her height increasing, and her very form transitioning into something very, very different. Bones stretched, tendons elongated, organs rearranged, and not a bit of it was painful, just fascinating, as was the end result.

Raine stared at herself in delight. "I'm a dragon!"

"Yes, my love," Weynild said, transforming into her own natural form. "You're a dragon."

"I'm a dragon!" Raine repeated. She was ecstatic. The possibilities were endless. She braced herself, then blew out a stream of fire that did not impress Weynild, and only slightly singed the bedding. "I can breathe fire," Raine said excitedly. She flapped her wings. "I can fly—"

"Yes," Weynild said drily, interrupting her. "Among other things."

"What—-?" Raine began, then caught the look from her lover, the one that was unmistakable in all her forms. "Oh," Raine said as her eyes turned dark violet, a color Weynild thought was fetching on a dragon and matched the deep purple of her scales.

Raine compared herself to Weynild. "Wait a minute," she said in dismay, "why am I so small?"

"Male dragons are generally smaller than female dragons," Weynild said, her tone even drier.

The violet eyes blinked at this revelation, and the purple wings gave an involuntary little flutter.

"You mean, I get to be the boy?"

"Yes, my love," Weynild said patiently. "You get to be the boy."

Epilogue 1

A dark figure moved through the halls of Ásgarðr, one whom all avoided if possible. Hel entered Sjöfn's chambers without being bidden to enter, and found the woman seated before her mirror brushing her long blonde hair. As Hel expected, Sjöfn looked at her unbidden entrance angrily, but did not say anything. She simply continued brushing her hair as Hel settled into the chair behind her, seemingly content to watch her perform her beauty regimen. At last, the Goddess of Love could stand it no longer and made eye contact with Hel in the mirror.

"What do you want, Hel?"

"Nothing," Hel said, the mildness of her response as unnerving as her manner. "Nothing at all."

"Then why are you here?"

The emerald eyes drifted around the room, examining the many beautiful artifacts, the vases filled with flowers, the lovely artwork and luxurious furniture. Although Sjöfn continued to brush her hair, Hel's examination took just long enough to put her completely on edge.

"I have been wracking my brain," Hel said, "trying to figure out why you and Tyr would seek to involve yourself in this matter," Her overly casual tone set off all sorts of alarms in Sjöfn. "Why you would seek to insert yourself in my affairs."

Sjöfn, said nothing, simply continued to brush her hair. But the brushing had slowed.

"And then it occurred to me," Hel said, picking at the embroidery on her chair. "I remember a time, oh, some three hundred odd years ago. Many lingering glances between you and Tyr, whispered conversations, the grazing of hands, always just out of sight of your respective spouses."

The brushing grew even slower.

"And then something else occurred to me."

Hel's mock bewilderment was wearing on her. Sjöfn stopped and set the brush on the table in front of her.

"What if?" Hel said, pausing for dramatic effect. "What if you and Tyr sparked a little something to life in your indiscretion?" Hel's mock bewilderment turned to mock horror. "Oh, I know how Tyr would react, so brutally pragmatic. He would want you to rid yourself of the evidence of your infidelity."

Sjöfn's jaw worked, but she said nothing, staring at the table in front of her.

"But you," Hel breathed out, pretending both pity and commiseration, "you would never be able to do such a thing. So soft-hearted." Hel took a moment to seemingly contemplate this impossible situation. "You would never be able to extinguish that light."

Sjöfn remained silent.

"So what if," Hel said slowly, "what if, instead, you sent that little spark to the mortal realm? To a couple incapable of having a child." Hel paused, reveling in her hypothesis and its conclusion. "To a couple who just happened to be the very epitome of Love and War."

It was enough for Sjöfn. Her eyes flickered upward to the Goddess of the Underworld and her tone was bitter. "What do you want, Hel?"

Hel held Sjöfn's gaze in the mirror, a smile playing about her lips.

"As I said before, nothing."

Hel's eyes and her tone hardened and she now made herself very clear. "This is not over. It is only just beginning, and in the future, I expect that you will not interfere."

She stood, and the Goddess of the Underworld gave the Goddess of Love one last volcanic look.

"In other words," Hel said, "I expect you to do—nothing."

Epilogue 2

Bruises covered Raine from one end of her body to the other, but every one of them had been gloriously acquired. She had been a dragon from sunset to sunset, a full night and day, and although she had flown and breathed fire, most of it had been spent mounting an insatiable fiery red dragon.

Although, Raine mused, Weynild hardly looked dissatisfied lying on her back in her human form in the great nest. In fact, she was not certain she had ever seen her love so completely sated. The golden eyes flicked over the bruises, taking inventory of the damage. One particularly large bruise on Raine's thigh caught her attention.

"I think I may have fractured your leg."

Raine shrugged. "It was well-worth it. Although it seems a bit perilous for the male dragon."

"The mortality rate is dangerously high," Weynild said, "you are far more hardy than most." She leaned to kiss the bruise nearest her.

Raine lay back down, content to stare upward at the hole in the ceiling of the cave, at the true stars of Arianthem. But her thoughts kept returning to the last few hours.

"By the gods, that was epic," she murmured, then grinned. "So that was your greatest heart's desire?"

"What?" Weynild said, surprised. "No, of course not, that was just means to an end."

"Means to an end?" Raine said, rolling over onto her side and leaning on her elbow. "What in the world could be better than—"

Suddenly, a multitude of things impressed themselves upon Raine. Weynild's deep contentment, the soft glow in her golden eyes, the way she rested her hand so protectively on her stomach.

"Wait," Raine said with incredulity. "Do you mean—?"

Weynild waited patiently for her to get a sentence out.

"You are—?"

Weynild still waited patiently.

"I mean, we are—?"

Weynild finally had mercy on her joyous companion.

"Yes, my love, we are."

Printed in Poland
by Amazon Fulfillment
Poland Sp. z o.o., Wrocław